UNIVERSAL DEFENDER
<BOOK 1>

Today I Save Myself

by Gregor Fjellrev

Blue Forge Press
Port Orchard, Washington

Universal Defender: Today I Save Myself (Book 1)
Copyright 2020, 2022
by Gregor Fjellrev

First eBook Edition March 2021
First Print Edition March 2021
Second eBook Edition February 2022
Second Print Edition February 2022

ISBN 978-1-59092-947-6

Cover design by Brianne DiMarco

Blue Forge Press is the print division of the volunteer-run, federal 501(c)3 nonprofit company, Blue Forge Group, founded in 1989 and dedicated to bringing light to the shadows and voice to the silence. We strive to empower storytellers across all walks of life with our four divisions: Blue Forge Press, Blue Forge Films, Blue Forge Gaming, and Blue Forge Records. Find out more at www.BlueForgeGroup.org

Blue Forge Press
7419 Ebbert Drive Southeast
Port Orchard, Washington 98367
blueforgepress@gmail.com
360-550-2071 ph.txt

My gift to you, Miles.
All the adventures and allies I'll never have.

MORE BY GREGOR FJELLREV

Universal Defender

Book 1: Today I Save Myself

Book 2: Fire to Burn the Stars

Book 3: Enter Unmaker

Blue Flash

Miles Radien and the Cult of the Chaosmaker
(Universal Defender)

Veralis Stratenheim and the Bridge Across Fire
(Universal Defender)

Reticent (Angels of Anarchy)

Talenostrum

Night of the Whapwolf

In Combat with Time

www.BlueForgePress.com

UNIVERSAL DEFENDER
<BOOK 1>

Today I Save Myself

BY GREGOR FJELLREV

CHAPTER THE FIRST

Miles Radien stood alone, but this was not a bad thing. While it was not good, it certainly was the standard, and he honestly wouldn't have it any other way. Miles understood the nature of the world, in that a friend is merely an ally who has yet to prove themselves your enemy, and the trick is to drift apart or die of old age before such an opportunity for betrayal presents itself. Alone does not mean lonely.

But that is not what Miles despaired over. He despaired over where he stood, rather than how he stood. He stood on Earth. A world he despised, full of a species of inherent spite, and a deliberate love of evil. The spite rubbed off on him, sure, but he would do all in his minuscule power to ensure that the evil aspect of humanity did not. Understanding one's own darkness, that it may be fought against, and subdued. At least, that was what he hoped he was doing.

Every day Miles went to the woods near his home, where only he lived. Like clockwork, around 6:00 PM, he'd sit in those woods, at the dried-up remnant of a creekbed, to sit there motionless, on his knees, and to close his eyes, blocking out the world around him. Hearing only the sound of silence, that slight ring of strangely relaxing harmonic, and even slowing his breathing to a crawl. He'd simply empty his mind of conscious thought, thinking only of the sound itself that was emptiness.

But something was different about today, when he went down to the woods. As he walked down the path, he couldn't help but feel as though something else was there. An animal, maybe? But these woods were nearly desolate of life, with only the occasional coyote in the midnight hours. And no human came to these woods anymore, let alone his secret hide. He wasn't about to be deterred, though. Once again, he sat at his spot. Once again, he closed his eyes and soon heard that serene humming that was the sound of silence.

A twig snapped.

Miles's eyes shot open, and he scrambled to his feet. He may not have been the best of fighters, but he had training enough to know what he was doing. Before him was a person, but... not quite? Whoever they were, they seemed out of place here, as if a spirit came to this world with only a basic knowledge of how a person looks when they're not suspicious.

Finally, Miles spoke. "I'd say 'who dares,' but that seems a little much. Even so, who are you?"

A moment passed before the figure spoke "You may call me Melaqros," this being said in a masculine voice, albeit seemingly as if a lizard was trying to speak it. He removed his hood as a grey mist barely encompassed him, shifting a human form to that of what almost appeared to be a... Komodo Dragon? Some kind of reptilian for sure, but he stood upright upon two legs. "I got your message."

"Message?" Miles inquired. "What are you on about? I don't have the technology to send messages. At least, not the kind that can call the attention of people like you."

Miles figured that this being was not of Earth, or any planet he knew. But whoever this was, he did not attack outright, so Miles was more than willing to hear him out.

Melaqros seemed confused. "Then what have been those fonts of pure cosmic power that have seethed from you every day for years? Do you... do you even know what emanates from you? A distress signal, to any who can listen!"

Miles stood stunned. What he was doing, that humming when all was silent, it was *that*? Cosmic power? Not even that, but *he* was capable of, let alone actively emitting it?

Melaqros looked around, seemingly nervous. "I haven't much time. Even now, the forces of your world move against me, simply for my presence. My ship is not far. We must—"

In most infuriating timing if not for its tragic nature, a *thip* sound was heard, then the report of a rifle, and Melaqros fell to his knees. Miles shouted and came to him, catching this creature before he would have fallen to his back, and taking him behind a nearby tree, for whatever it may have been worth. These old, dead trees would make for lousy cover. "I... I don't know where your people keep their internal organs, but I don't know how to save you, or even if I can."

"No time for me, I've run my course," Melaqros said, reaching into the pocket of the brown jacket he wore, and placing something in Miles's hand. "My ship isn't far. Take it, put this in, it will bring you to Cynofrax, where you will find your answers upon The Mountain. There is so much about the universe you don't yet know, but you will. Today, you must save yourself, so tomorrow you might save your world, and in time... all of creation."

Melaqros went limp in Miles's arms, and soon after fell apart to dust. Not quite dust, rather, but... sparks?

"Well, that solves the issue of leaving a body for the government to dissect," Miles said. But the sentiment was short lived as he heard shouting, and looked in his hand to see a triangular sort of 'key,' glowing a deep blue. "Ok, you gotta help me here..."

As if it knew what he sought, a blue shimmer passed over the empty air and revealed a craft clearly far beyond Earth's technology. The cockpit opened, awaiting its pilot. Or at least, his replacement. Miles ran to the ship, and heard someone yell "Stop him!" as he did so. A gunshot was heard and a bullet pinged off the plating of the craft, and another order barked. "No! We need the specimen intact!" Miles, with his cue to leave, hastily crawled into the cockpit of the ship, which closed automatically.

"Alright then, where does this thing go?" Miles said to himself, and soon saw a red-glowing slot in the console, perfectly shaped to the device he held in his hand. He placed the key into the slot, and the ship hummed to life.

"Coordinates accepted, preparing warp to Cynofrax," an automated voice said, to Miles's surprise. How did it know what to say to him in English? The ship blasted off, away from the now-insignificant suits below, and soon was beyond Earth orbit. A countdown started to warp, and Miles braced himself. The ship jumped forth into warp, but surprisingly, Miles felt no kickback. "The wonders of... whatever technology this is, I guess."

It was only a matter of minutes before the ship exited warp, and Miles beheld a planet not unlike the kind he saw in movies in books. It seemed... too incredible to be real. The sheer splendor of it seemed as though it belonged in the realm of fiction, but there it was. Cynofrax. He hoped. The ship landed itself on an open plain, and the cockpit hissed open. To his surprise, Miles was able to breathe this air.

However, any admiration of where he stood was quickly cut short when an armored individual started running towards him, a rifle of some design in his hands. *"Ike-Duul?"* the creature yelled. *"Thra-Duulen!"*

With no clue what else to do, and also unsure of what he was expecting when he suddenly landed on a planet like this, Miles put his hands up. "I don't know what you're saying! This ship flew me here on its own!"

The armored being stopped, and waited for a moment, before responding. "Who are you, and why did you land here? Craft aren't to land on the Plains of the Stars, not even in emergency!"

Now more confused than ever as to how this

person suddenly spoke English, Miles figured just answering its questions would be better than asking his own. "My name is Miles Radien, and I wasn't controlling the ship. It piloted itself here after someone gave me the key, telling me I needed to find my answers on Cynofrax, which I really hope this planet is!"

"Then where is the pilot now?"

"He was killed by natives on the planet, my kinsmen, who I hold no pride for. I can only assume he intended to take me here himself, but that became impossible. Do you recognize this craft, and know who the pilot is?"

The armored individual pressed a button on the neck plating of his suit, and the helmet retracted itself to reveal that this person was more akin to a fox standing on two legs, with some incredibly heightened intelligence. "I suppose you are owed some answers, as you've given them to me. My name is Arakai, and this is indeed Cynofrax, homeworld of the Vulpian people. The ship you arrived in, and admittedly parked illegally is known as The Aura Runner. Its pilot was never known, as the ship had only ever been... told stories of. A ship of myth, as it were. If you would allow me, I will place a device on it that will pilot it to a more legal landing platform."

Miles stood aside and allowed Arakai to place a

small circular piece of metal on The Aura Runner, and it took off towards one of the grand cities in the distance. "Don't worry, I will ensure the ship is back in your hands when you leave. If what you say is true, and the pilot gave you its Chronokey willingly, it belongs to you now."

A moment passed before Miles spoke. "But what now? That guy... the one who gave me the ship said he had come because I was giving off some kind of cosmic distress signal. I didn't even know I could do that. Before he died, he said something about saving myself today, to save my world tomorrow, and eventually the whole of creation. Do you have any idea what he might've been on about?"

Arakai stopped for a moment. "I don't know for sure, but I recommend you visit The Aura Prism on The Mountain. And before you ask, it's the only mountain on Cynofrax, so it doesn't need a name beyond The Mountain. If you need quick passage to it, this town we're not far from should have someone willing to get you there, for a price. Usually work or favors."

Miles felt like he was on a quest from a video game that presented itself as a paltry side-errand, but would suddenly open up into a storyline bigger than the one claiming to be the 'main' one. But that wasn't a bad thing for him. It was something he'd dreamed about for so long. All his life, he was the loner, the one playing in the backyard on his own, waving a stick around at the air, and only getting to imagine what it all meant. Countless adventures across the worlds and the stars, defeating the most evil of foes, and sorting fair play across the cosmos, forging the strongest of alliances, and bringing light to the darkest corners of creation. All the worlds he imagined in his head, he just might get to see them finally. He'd get to live the dream that haunted him for his whole life. Miles even wondered if some of the things he imagined about would turn up in his own adventures. But that was for later. Now, he needed to get to this mountain. The Mountain, as it were.

Following Arakai into the town called Kaldres-Viane, he took the Vulpian's recommendation and entered what looked to be the local bar, but it had a more tavern sort of atmosphere than anything else. Travelers from across the stars instead of just one world, swapping stories and having just a damn good time of their lives. Miles looked around, and approached the bar counter itself. While having the atmosphere of a tavern, it was clear that there was some very clever technology at work here. Soon, the Vulpian barkeep was ready to hear what he had to say.

"I don't know if any language I speak works here," Miles said, to which the barkeep held his hand up as if to say 'Just a moment,' before telling him in plain

English that he was ready. "Right," Miles continued. "I've been told I need to get to The Mountain, and that someone might be able to help me with passage there. I can pay in manual labor or protection, I have some training in combat, enough to protect myself. It might be enough, but I don't know for sure."

Miles wasn't lying. He did have experience in Martial Arts, particularly Eskrima and Savate Kickboxing, as well as dabbling in Historical European Martial Arts.

"I don't know about manual labor, let alone protection. But if you have experience playing an instrument of some kind, you'll be the most popular guy in town. This place and its regulars have been starved of a good musician. Usually we keep getting uppity types who talk more about their cosmic inspiration for a given song than they actually play it for..." The barkeep's ears flattened at making that point, clearly he had remembered a few painfully boring people like that.

"Well, I can play an instrument, but I'm not sure anyone here's heard of it. Only because I'm so very much not from around here. Hell, the bastards I call my kinsmen can barely get to the next planet over, and that's not counting just how much of scum they are as beings."

"There's a Replicator over there," the barkeep said as he pointed at what looked more like a space-age photo booth. "It will be able to use your memories of playing the instrument to construct one for you. As for how colorfully you describe your own species, that's an interesting stance to take to one's own kind."

"If you knew them, you'd say worse than I do," Miles said as he headed towards the Replicator. He placed his hand on a small circular panel, and soon, a guitar of the same make and model as his personal one had materialized itself in front of him, and even an amp to spare with the associated cables. "Well, that's quite clever, then. I suppose whatever passes as an outlet will be adaptable too?"

Sure enough, when Miles needed to plug the amp itself into a wall socket, a different circular panel (silver rather than blue) morphed itself around the prongs of the plug. He then checked the tuning of the guitar. Standard tuning, like his usual. After turning the amp on and setting it to a heavy distortion, the kind for hard rock and metal, he turned around and saw that all eyes were on him, eagerly awaiting whatever he was about to do.

"I feel like I'm about to be praised or killed, and the next few moments will decide which," Miles said, which incited some laughter among the crowd. Now knowing his audience and that they could understand him, Miles played a few practice notes, before jumping into a set of covers from classic rock and metal artists he always enjoyed, and the tavern goers certainly enjoyed them too. Twisted Sister's "We're Not Gonna Take It" in particular was a hit. After that, he decided it was a good time to show one of his originals. One he called "Song of the Defender". It had no lyrics, so its notes did the talking. And it was a rousing success, to say the least. Clearly, he was a welcome break from whatever was passing for a musician around here for the past while.

After the set, Miles put the guitar into the replicator, and it, along with the amp and the cables dissolved, likely to be re-assembled into something new another time. Many were already offering to buy him drinks, and he was willing to oblige, so long as they didn't dissolve his stomach. Surprisingly, the range of brews and libations were quite similar to what he found on Earth, just under different names. It seemed the best way to find what he was looking for was to simply say its base ingredient along with 'brew' or 'distillate'. It's what got him a glass of something called 'Gelvetori Doomrye,' and it certainly was. A single glass had the effect of maybe three of regular Earth whisky. But Miles wasn't a lightweight, and was only just buzzed after it.

A Vulpian approached him as he washed the Doomrye down with some water and a plate of something called Kynvalt, a dish not from Cynofrax, but a planet called Varenthiil, described as "Fried

Fleischberries". It tasted like fried bear meat; akin to beef, but more gamey. "Your playstyle is a welcome break from the types we tend to get around here," she complimented.

"So I've figured," Miles replied. "I've dealt with the types you seem to describe, and they are insufferable."

"Gods, I know!" she said, almost excited that Miles could relate. "They take up more time just talking than actually playing! 'Oh, this song was inspired by the something fields of some ridiculous planet that I was on vacation on with an overblown budget, and spent the whole time sipping only the *finest* drink, and the *most choice* of foods…" She paused for a moment. "Even with that much sarcasm, that physically hurt to say."

Miles snorted upon her saying 'finest' in such an exaggerated tone, nearly spitting his water out. "I have never in my life related to someone more than now, I think."

The two laughed, and the Vulpian sat down at the bar, pondering what drink to down in seconds, just to make up for a painfully spot-on impression of someone who represents what's wrong with the universe. Miles pondered for a second before speaking up.

"Have they got mead here?" he asked. "Honey wine?" Miles's new friend nodded, ordering one for each of them, and soon both had tankards in hand.

"We never did properly introduce ourselves," she said. "Veralis Stratenheim." And raised her drink.

"Miles Radien."

The two started to down the mugs, and their contents, staring at each other the whole time, wondering who was going to do the successful one-up. It ended up a tie, and both slammed their mugs on the bar counter. "Damn, but that's good!" Miles exclaimed.

"No argument here!" Veralis added, and they both laughed. Almost two hours passed as Miles finished his food and chatted with Veralis. It was honestly the most conversation he'd had in months, and likely the only one he'd ever enjoyed partaking in. It didn't matter that Veralis wasn't human, and that some wisecracks had been lost on both sides of things every now and again, but it just seemed right to have a good conversation with a good person. Or Vulpian, as it were. But Miles found it odd, how quickly he was accepted here on Cynofrax. For the longest time, he imagined that across the universe, calling someone 'Human-like' would be an insult enough to warrant a fight to the death. That his people were the exemplar of inherent evil in an entire species, even with the vastness of the universe. He had even asked Veralis and a few others if they had heard of his species, and got no answer.

"So, what's on your mind, then?" Veralis asked of Miles, seeing him ponder the strangeness of him not being dead yet for his species.

"It's just... I hope you don't think of me as the average of my race. I mean that in the way of that any other human is as... tolerable as me," Miles responded.

Veralis tilted her head slightly, clearly confused.

"The Humans of Earth... the ones I've always hated being among, they're evil. They're a species of liars, backstabbers, and cowards with hearts as black as the void between galaxies."

"So what does that make you?"

"I remember a wise man once said 'a person is smart, people are dumb, panicky animals.' At this point, I'm the only one of my kind who's ever been to a planet other than Earth, let alone so far out here, meeting all these new peoples. But I know that as a species, the Humans could never be trusted with the knowledge of this wider universe."

Veralis sipped her replacement drink. "But that doesn't answer my question. What does that make you? An exception? If all your kind is evil save for you, then how do you know it's not the opposite?"

"I know and understand my own nature, that I don't do good things as a good person, but to hold back my inner darkness, the darkness that all Humans have. I know my enemy, this inherent evil, and thus I know how to fight it. To subdue it, if not defeat and destroy it. Make no mistake, Veralis. You've no reason to trust me, and you'd be right to not. I wonder if that Melaqros guy was just fucking with me, and decided to show the universe to me, and fake his death so he could watch me have a good time before taking it away. Probably by knocking me out and taking me back to Earth, make me think it was all a dream. Another fantasy."

As soon as Miles mentioned the name Melaqros, Veralis's ears perked up. "Melaqros? Is that the name he used?"

"Aye. Did you know him?"

"Melaqros isn't the name of a person. It's a word in Draconic, literally meaning 'out of time'. It's not a word used lightly by any of the Draconic peoples. Only when one knows he or she is about to die do they use that word to name themselves in those last moments, and to make their last requests and arrangements. If a Dragon of some kind called himself Melaqros, and gave you his ship, he knew he was dying, and he knew there was something about you that needed saving before it was too late."

Miles looked over to Veralis, the look of solemn preparation to face reality replaced with intrigue, and maybe even a little hope that the universe isn't that cruel.

"Trust me Miles, no Dragon would call themselves Melaqros in any other situation. Even the most manipulative of despots and tricksters didn't use that word as part of a sick prank."

A moment passed before Veralis spoke again. "You need to get to The Mountain, don't you?" Miles nodded. "He told you to find answers at The Mountain?" She seemed almost ecstatic for some reason. "Then once those drinks wear off, it would be my honor to take you there to meet The Aura Prism!"

CHAPTER THE SECOND

Miles spent the night at Veralis's home in Kaldres-Viane, sleeping off the few drinks he had, so he could be in optimal shape to meet The Aura Prism. When he woke up that morning, he was ready to simply be in his own bed at his home, seeing that this was just a cruel dream. But that was not the case. He woke up in the guest room Veralis showed him, on Cynofrax.

For it, he felt happy for the first time in his life he could remember. Maybe he'd been happy before, but that was before he could keep memories. As little as it seemed, just to wake up today, it meant the universe to him. To show that at long last, he had escaped. Finally, he could declare a victory. It wasn't just a dream, and that made him happy.

Miles looked out the nearby window upon the town of Kaldres-Viane, and sighed in satisfied relief. He bowed his head slightly at the scene before him, as if to thank all of the powers that may have finally let him stand where he did.

"Just let me know when you're ready," Veralis's voice said from outside the room.

"Whenever you are," Miles replied.

Not long after, the two were on their way. Veralis said that the ship he arrived in would be at the Starport at Sorrenikas, as it was the closest major city to Kaldres-Viane. She also assured that it was policy that in situations like Miles's, his ship would be moved to a place at the nearest major Starport. Coincidentally, Sorrenikas was the city they would head to in order to get to The Mountain, as it was along the Kandorian Sound that allowed for easy passage to The Mountain. Soon, the two had arrived at the water-port of Sorrenikas, and Veralis quickly was able to spot someone able to get them to The Mountain reasonably. Miles, of course, trusted her judgment on this matter, seeing as he was the foreigner here. A short boat ride later, and the two stood at the base of The Mountain, a tunnel leading directly into the stone itself, and stairs spiraling upwards.

"Those stairs go all the way to the peak," Veralis explained. "You may have wondered why this place isn't full of people. Tourists, looking to sneak a peek at the Prism, so-called sages and wisemen, hoping to ask questions of it. It's because those stairs are are the most they see. They try to enter this tunnel, and cannot. They are blocked by an impenetrable force field, and only those that the Prism is expecting to see can do so. This is the final test, as it were. If that Dragon told you to come here, and to seek the Prism, you should be able to do so. I can't go further, I've already had my meet with it to gain access to the power it guards."

Miles looked over to Veralis. "The power it guards?"

"The Cosmic Powers are known by many names. Some call it Chainbreaker, others know it as the *Thuul* or the *Kaln*, or any number of words. To the Vulpian peoples, we name it The Aura. Those with the ability to tap into the ever-present current of energy that is all things have on occasion become the greatest heroes the universe has known, while others simply live for untold years as they travel and participate in the grand scale of reality. Sometimes they just live normal lives, and use power to aid in just... living. Some, very few are born inherently able to tap into power, others train themselves to do so. For many, they must pass a trial to be granted the capability to draw power. It's what I did."

"Then I should quit making the Prism wait," Miles

said as he walked towards the tunnel's entrance, and placed a single foot inside. He discovered no obstacle. The Aura Prism indeed awaited, and Miles had no plans to let it down.

The stairs themselves didn't seem to tire Miles as much as he thought they might. Perhaps some power kept his stamina going. Perhaps he was just too excited. Either way, he pressed forth, albeit in near total darkness. He could only see the steps themselves, and even then, only their outline. The walls of the tunnel itself were pitch-black, and maybe even vastly far away, perhaps this climb was far more precarious than Miles was giving it credit for.

Suddenly, a spark seemed to shoot across the dark wall, and Miles whipped around to look. Nothing followed, so he kept going, until another spark crossed his vision. Miles tried to find where it went as he continued stepping up and up, but he could only ever catch these wayward lights in his peripheral vision. The corners of his eyes soon danced with light, more present than before, and a voice... didn't boom in the darkness, but it's presence was made known.

"Miles, Human of Earth," it said.

"Aye, that's me," he replied, almost disappointed in its truth.

"I do not make a habit of theatrics, so I say to you

something you've known, but never told: This is not the first time you have beheld a power beyond your world."

Miles would've frozen, but he kept climbing the stairs, despite how his heart skipped a beat. But he could not lie now. "Aye," he finally said. "But I never knew that this was what I saw."

"Then tell me, what did you see, and what did you make of it?"

"You already know the answer."

"But you still should give it, for your sake more than mine."

"I've dreamed of this moment. And I don't entirely mean that I've fantasized of it, nor do I mean this exact moment. But all my life, I've had visions and dreams of other worlds. Other planets, stars, peoples, galaxies…"

Miles felt he may have stood still right there, but he kept moving. Not because something made him, but because his unconscious body knew that this needed to happen, and had no intention to delay it, let alone stop.

"Never an exact world, but the idea of it. Never the name of a species or a person, but the raw concept of what or who they are. A universe born of my mind's eye, and all the dreams I've had of living in it. And in a way, I did."

"Don't cease now, Radien," the voice

encouraged. Miles figured it had to be that of The Aura Prism.

"I spent my whole life seeing and imagining these worlds, and the adventures I'd have on them. I acted them out in my own backyard, with a piece of broken wooden dowel to pretend was my sword against the dark forces of Creation. In the eyes of the world, I was just a kid waving around a stick. But in my eyes... I held a blade of incredible power, and with it, I fought the most fearsome of foes, wandered many planets, walked all kinds of lives. I imagined my powerful allies, and the good for all Reality we did."

Finally, Miles did stop. Then, he let out a great sigh.

"But sooner or later, I had to wake up, as it were. For all that wonderful fantasy, there was still a reality that had to be gone back to. To trudge through, to suffer the weight of. Even now... I wonder when I'm going to wake up."

All the sparks faded.

"Miles, Human of Earth," The Prism said again. "That is a title with no place being the one you bear."

Suddenly, Miles found himself atop the mountain, facing a great prismatic gem of deep, swirling blue, well over twice his height. "There is no dream to wake from anymore. You stand at the cusp of the universe you always wanted to explore."

"So, what's the catch?" Miles asked.

"The catch is that you believe there is one." The Prism's voice echoed in Miles's head. "I will not deny that it is a consequence of your upbringing, surrounded by countless twisted, manipulative souls. You seek out what catch there is because you know one always exists, and in your defense, one always has. All your life, you've needed to scrutinize every word, either ones that you said, or were said by another, for you knew that the slightest fault, the most minuscule slivers of what could be seen as weakness would be mercilessly exploited and battered upon. A world where the only true goal, the only cause that could ensure your thriving was to exploit and destroy all others that did not meet and further your own. What does that sound like to you?"

"That sounds like Earth," Miles stated with barely any hesitation.

"What planet do you stand on now?"

"I stand on Cynofrax."

"How many planets called Earth contain Humans?"

"Only one that I know."

"Of all the planets and all the stars, the Humans of Earth are the only ones I've ever seen that would ruin a good thing and enjoy it, thinking it was the right thing to do. They exist on one planet, and one planet only as it stands. You are only Human in body, Miles. You heart, your mind, your very soul... They belong to another race. Which exactly, I cannot say. Only you will be able to, in time. But beyond any doubt, I can guarantee you, not by destiny, but simply by what I know of the universe... You will be far, far greater than a Human could ever dream of being. Because even your dreams aren't Human. They're anyone else, from anywhere else."

Miles had never heard such things said to him before. Even with the unfortunate truth some of them did bear, his spirit still never felt more lifted by just how right he was all along, and how it will finally save him.

"I offer you the power you've deserved, and gone without for too long. I offer you The Aura. Your friend Veralis, she will teach you how to wield it. To temper power with wisdom, as she has over her years. You, like her, will become ageless, time will never wither you. You will be hyper-regenerative, able to heal any wound naturally in moments. So long as a single cell of your being remains, you can regrow your entire body, and you consciousness will remain intact. You will undergo a process known as True Physical Optimization, wherein your body will enter the peak physical fitness it possibly can as it stands. Excess energy, such as fat, or whatever waste you may produce will simply be absorbed to fuel this regenerative nature you will gain. You still, of course, can eat, drink, or rest, but it no longer is required to survive. And to top that off, you will be granted Universal Understanding, wherein you shall be able to speak and understand any language spoken to you, this ability will evolve as languages do so naturally."

Miles felt his heart practically rise in his chest as the Prism made this incredible offer.

"The Aura is that, and so much more, as you will discover in your journey."

"I shall gladly accept your offer, Prism of The Aura," Miles declared. Almost instantly after, he felt something hit his chest, and spread through his body, like the tingling sensation one experiences when listening to epic orchestral music. It was as if his entire being flowed with raw power, and... was he being lifted into the air? He was! Only about six inches, but there was no mistake. This raw energy that flowed through him, its power was unquestionable. His feet touched the ground again, and he righted himself, and held his left hand in front of him.

With a snap of his fingers, a deep blue flame ignited in his hand. He closed his fist, and the flame went out. He couldn't even explain to himself what he did to make it happen. It wasn't a thought, a command... he just *knew* that's what he needed to do.

"I owe you a debt I can never repay," Miles

finally spoke.

"Your deeds will decide that," The Prism told him. "You may be immortal, but you are not invincible. You can still die, but it would practically have to be by your own will. Your form will adjust to your power."

With that same *just knowing* that lit a flame in his hands, Miles warped to the base of The Mountain, where Veralis was waiting for him. As soon as he appeared before her, she smiled.

"I know that look, because that was my look years ago."

CHAPTER THE THIRD

eralis and Miles headed back to her home in Kaldres-Viane, and the Vulpian set up a straw target for him. "Let's see what you can do," she said. "And mostly, I mean 'You should see what you can do now.'"

Miles looked to the target a good thirty paces away, and thrust his left palm towards it. A bolt of white power blasted from his hand and struck the target, blowing it to shreds. Miles was ecstatic, laughing in joy that he could do something he found impressive now! It wasn't the fact he blew up a target that mattered to him, but that it was a literal power he wielded, and could call upon! Out of curiosity, he made a turning motion with his hand, and that same *knowing* concentration that gave him a flame, and a bolt now reassembled the target, as if it had never been struck in the first place.

Miles cheered, hooting and hollering, running in circles, in a state of pure euphoria that this was what he could do now. The responsibility he knew he'd have to adopt wasn't what was on his mind, he believed in himself. But just even that... he believed in himself! That was never something he did before!

"By all the stars, and all the worlds... it's real! It's all real!" he finally said to Veralis, before hugging her tightly, to her surprise, but not her protest. "Thank you! Thank you so much!" His eyes watered with pure joy. Veralis placed a handpaw on his head; she was eight inches taller than him, after all. "There won't be a day I regret this!"

"And I'll bet there's so many things you've done today and are doing right now that you never believed could be," Veralis calmly said.

"Hell, I'm not a hugging person," Miles said once he finally let her go. "But that can change now! I could be that kind of person now! I've got reason to be! At long last, I've got a reason to *be*!"

The ecstasy lasted for the whole day, before Miles calmed down in the mid-evening.

"So," Veralis started. "What first?"

"Gods, I'm not even sure!" Miles responded, then

thought for a few moments, when he calmly answered. "Now that I think of it, there's some loose ends I need to tie up on Earth, if you can believe it."

"Well, don't let me stop you!" Veralis said. "Unless of course, you start being an ass about your power."

"Honestly, I should take some time to get used to it," Miles acknowledged. "Maybe figure out some standards of proceeding, limits on what I do, when I do it, and how."

"It may even be a good idea to just take that time regardless, and your adventures will come to you. Seeking out that kind of thing rarely ends favorably."

"Aye. I'll make sure I temper this power with wisdom."

With that same *knowing*, Miles warped himself all the way back to Earth. He knew where he needed to be in the universe, and clearly this power had intuition, and no malintent. Not like a djinni who'll give you *exactly what you have asked for*, and have that screw you over. He knew where he needed to be, and so did The Aura. Back in those woods near his home, he felt another power nearby. Miles walked over to the source, which happened to be where he sat and did his pseudo-meditation for however many years he did. That power was indeed a more primal and uncontrolled form of what he had now. And just as that Dragon calling himself Melaqros said, it felt like a distress call. A prayer for escape. Of course, Miles then quickly warped back into his own home, remembering the suits that were closing in on him when he was last on Earth.

The house had a very... odd sort of undisturbed feel to it. Everything was in its proper place, exactly as he had left it. But it didn't feel correct. Yes, all of his little DIY projects were exactly as they were supposed to be, but Miles couldn't shake the feeling that something was not right with them. Miles concentrated, activating his power to try to see just what had changed...

The house was lined with bugs. Microcameras and hidden audio recorders, practically in every wall of the house, as if whoever was watching them was waiting for Miles to reveal a hidden purpose to it all, a secret lair or bunker or whatever.

Thus, Miles simply turned around and walked back outside. He kept his alert up, showing that indeed, there was a car parked in the culdesac containing undercover operatives of... something. It didn't matter much to Miles who they were, only the fact that they were there. But it was clear whoever they were, they were much better at subtlety than a federal-issue goon. The car was an older model Civic, and the faint smell of marijuana was certainly present, much like how students from the local high school would cut class or leave early to hotbox themselves in that very culdesac. But not only had this Civic never been in the culdesac before, and even though whoever was there was indeed surrounding themselves with the smoke of weed, they were there for Miles, and knew that, even if senses were dulled and appetites were enhanced.

Miles still walked out of his neighborhood, and towards the local pub. Not as divey as one might expect, but definitely the kind of place you'd go for a few pints and not much else. But he skipped the pub, heading instead into the bakery next door, run by a Ukrainian family. He didn't speak Ukrainian, but that may very well have changed after acquiring The Aura, and the Universal Understanding that the Prism told him about. Miles did still have a fair bit of cash in his wallet, so he could grab some tarragon soda if nothing else. He grabbed the liter-and-a-half glass bottle and brought it to the checkout.

"Just this one again?" the cashier asked in English.

"Well, unless you got a liquor license and have Slivovitz now, I'm afraid not," Miles replied, to her surprise. Something in Miles's head made him understand that he was talking now in her native language of Ukrainian.

"I didn't know you spoke Ukrainian," she replied in kind. "And personally, I prefer Medovukha."

"Fair enough." The rest of that casual conversation was just as such, and Miles paid and left, opening the bottle and taking a drink. Tarragon soda was about his favorite non-alcoholic drink. On Earth, at least, he figured now that he'd start having to take into account different planetary specialties.

Once again, he knew something was off. While there were people definitely in the local element, they just weren't *from* here. Locals that didn't exist till yesterday, as it were. It was at this moment Miles realized he had absolutely zero plan for dealing with whoever killed Melaqros, and whoever is giving him the willies, likely the same entity.

Miles figured it would be a very stupid plan, what he was about to do, but at least it would be unexpected. Using The Aura to figure out which car belonged to whatever shady agency was following him, Miles then approached that car, and knocked on the driver's side window. It rolled down, and Miles looked at the driver, who still did a good job at looking like he belonged, but The Aura did not lie.

"I don't like being followed," Miles said. "If there's something you want to know from me, it's best to ask first, and then do the shady shit if that doesn't work."

Some time later, Miles and this organization that

identified itself as ETAL-RARC (pronouncing itself "ey-tal rawrk", and at the very least not having a tortured acronym clearly worked backwards from) found a neutral ground to meet at. Miles awaited the representative they were sending patiently, and eventually, she arrived.

"Mr. Radien, I represent the Extraplanetary Technologies and Lifeform Research and Response Commission, my name is Malin Teralce. We decided to begin keeping an eye on you due to your association with a non-earth creature, and the use of its technology."

"Ms. Teralce, the being you refer to as an 'it' was a 'he,' and had a name that I would've known had you not shot him dead."

"That shot was not fired from any of our operatives," Malin cut in sternly as Miles had to her. "Please, just hear me out on this. I'm not going to say we're not the bad guys, because then you'll never believe me on it. But just... please, let me tell you what we know of what happened."

Miles awaited her explanation.

"ETAL-RARC has only been in operation as a funded organization for maybe ten years. Before then, it was practically a backyard club of people who could talk sci-fi mumbo-jumbo, and guys smart enough to actually tinker with high-level technology. About those ten years ago, one of those founding members successfully made what he called an Energy Scanner, which picked up something astoundingly odd, and really hasn't stopped." She paused for a moment, taking what was likely a more refined version of the device from her pocket and putting it on the table between them. "We had to bullshit under oath to federal funding boards to get the money to actually figure out if this reading was legit, because even we didn't know for sure. But we had to say we knew it was odd, and needed to know more."

Malin placed a file folder on the table as well, and motioned for Miles to take a look, which he did. It showed the plans for what indeed would pick up energetic signatures of almost any kind, but not how to interpret such signals.

"We've been looking for that time for someone who can figure out how to better tell us: What is that energy, is it anything, how can we follow up on it? Whether that's harness power, or prepare defense, ETAL-RARC has been in the dark on that for a decade. Then the scanner picked up something new, and it was coming from where you were witnessed taking off in a clearly alien ship."

Miles used The Aura to scan the room for bugs and recording devices. To his surprise, there were none. So he decided he would tell his story, with a few details left out for his own safety.

"I walked to the woods near my home, basically a daily ritual of mine to just sit there and... sort of meditate. The day of the incident, a non-earth being calling himself Melaqros approached me, warning me of shady enemies and events to come to Earth. He even told me that Melaqros wasn't his name, but a word in his language, and he must've had some scoop I didn't know about, but he didn't get to say much. A bullet later, and he was dead, and then simply, fell apart, as if his own body had a defense against leaving itself behind to be torn apart for research and weaponization. Considering the time between the impact and report of the shot, he would've been three-quarters of a mile away at most. He gave me the... key of sorts to his ship, and told me to get out of there. I put the key where it looked like it was supposed to go, and the ship went into orbit, and cloaked itself. Apparently, that key also had some kind of mechanism to help me pass the time, because something knocked me out till a few hours ago, and I came back to my home to see what goons raided it, only to find how unnervingly undisturbed it was. Now I'm here because I was right."

Malin stood for a moment, wondering if there was lie in Miles's eyes. But The Aura was passively making sure no physical clues were given, and Miles couldn't be called out.

"So you're not an extraplanetary organism?" Miles nodded. "Not an established ally of this Melaqros fellow? Those frequencies I showed you from that Energy Scanner, do you even know what they are? I told my men to follow you because I thought you could identify them, that you could help!"

"Ms. Teralce, I don't know how much help I can be to you. But I can try," Miles said. "If you think I'm from another world, you'd be wrong. I wild-ass guessed my way into making that ship work for me off of what Melaqros told me, and I'm lucky to have been right." He paused for a moment. "But if you want my help, you must let me help in the way that I deem necessary. I can't have your men following me, I can't have you slipping bugs in my pockets, because believe me, I will know, and I will not take it well. I knew that there were exactly twenty-six cameras and microphones in my house, and that the old Civic in the culdesac was yours. I approached your men in their vehicle to meet with you. If you think you can pull anything over my eyes, you will learn harshly how that is not the case."

Malin sighed and rolled her shoulders. "I don't much like the pseudo-threat, and I hate to admit you're right. You pointed our boys out, as if you knew they were there before they planned to be. But don't let this make you think we won't be vigilant."

"I'm not expecting you to be complacent, Malin. I'm expecting you to not be shitty." Miles stood up, and prepared to walk out of the 'abandoned' office building.

"Miles?" Malin said. "If you find out what that energy is, what we're dealing with..." Miles stopped and looked back. "Don't tell us we can harness it. Don't make it look like we can use it. Between you and me, none of us can be trusted. Not even me, now matter how much I might tell myself."

Miles sighed. "I know. But if nothing else, you are wise to know it as well."

"Twenty-six cameras exactly, huh? I didn't even know that was the number. My men just put them where they were needed." Malin picked up the energy scanner and pointed it at Miles, and its readout showed a new frequency. "Whatever happened in that ship, something about you has fundamentally changed. You're exuding energy of some kind, and I've read and watched enough sci-fi and fantasy to just *know* that you can wield it. And God, I hope you can be trusted with it."

"So do I."

Miles stepped out of sight of the neutral ground building he and Malin met within, and warped himself elsewhere, this time to a stretch of highway in Minnesota between towns. Hard prairie for sure, nearest town: a considerable distance. The perfect place to set a sort of traveler's stop, or maybe a secret bunker. Perhaps both. Miles always did want to open a traveler's stop.

A few cans and scraps of litter were the only landmarks here, and you could almost see the curvature of the Earth itself. With The Aura, Miles tried to find out who owned the land on either side of the highway. All that surrounded him was just owned by the county or the state, and as long as he could last on it for long enough, he could probably even claim it without dispute. The prairie plains stretched out before him, only divided by the highway, and then he began to concentrate.

The Aura began to do its work, to create him a base to operate within. The litter of the plastic bags and aluminum cans began to collect and coalesce, even reforge the very atoms that made their existence. Atomic Reassignment. Rapid nuclear fission and fusion, whose explosive releases were being contained and re-used to fuel further processes, and even some of the ground itself was being pulled up and turned anew. As this went along, no cars drove down this stretch of lonely road to behold what Miles was doing, and soon metal became stone, became brick and mortar that built a structure, looking exactly like a family-run highway pit stop between towns. With this structure and the ground beneath it completed to their needs, Miles walked into its basement, and had a few ideas.

He warped himself to a nearby landfill, and warped himself back to this new base location with over two tons of trash and waste, and used The Aura to once again rearrange their atomic structures, pulling protons and neutrons apart and putting them back together, chaining them in compounds and chemicals that made molecules and structure. It took almost half that pile itself, but Miles soon had created a generator to power this base of his, a central catalystic crystal, a pylon of sorts, projecting raw electrical energy to power lights, equipment, tools, anything. Re-arranging more and more trash, the structure was now wired electrically, and lights were installed, and even furnishings were created to give it aesthetic life. Like a gas station convenience store, and a restaurant right inside as well. Miles figured he'd stock the place with stuff he'd just buy proper, with money likely gained from turning this trash quite literally into its weight in gold.

A bit of research and action later, and this little base of his not only served as a traveler's stop, but even could be the front he needed to be his operations on Earth, while he stayed here to learn more the limits and rules of his power of The Aura. By the end of the week, it was even stocked, and the rest of that trash had been turned into gold bullion and either sold or stored.

Miles considered it fortunate that the

circumstances that would lead to him doing something, that 'adventure' as one might call it did not present itself while he got this base and business ready, and even had it licensed by the state of Minnesota as a grocery store with a restaurant, permitted to serve alcohol in accordance with state guidelines, that he'd run entirely himself. That traveler's stop he always wanted to open was now real, and even with the ridiculous name he always wanted for it: The Fourteen Werewolves.

CHAPTER THE FOURTH

With the remainder of that trash pile, Miles had also constructed for himself a supercomputer unlike any other on Earth, and with The Aura, programmed its AI to learn and adapt to his speech patterns and requests, so that it could not only think, but reason and interpret. The process was rocky at first, but after about a week, it had a basic understanding of what Miles was after when he asked for something, and its learning code would only allow it to improve over time.

"Techbooth, activate," Miles would say at night when he wanted to get to work, or just between customers at the traveler's stop, which was anywhere from hours to days. The place served its purpose: A way station along the highway, in case one needed it. The double monitors would switch on at his voice key, and were ready to do what was needed.

"How's that analysis of the Energy Scanner's signature?" he asked, referring to the one that Malin showed him months ago. The Techbooth had been trying since then to figure it out, while learning its own ropes.

"The actual wavelength and frequency is vague at best, due to the primitive nature of the scanner used to find it."

Miles thought for a moment. "Can you cross-reference it with non-terrestrial sources? A sort of galactic network, if that's a thing?"

"Subwave tapping frequency does detect a 'galactic network,' as you describe. However, it seems to be locked from this planet's access under something described as "Conclave of Sentience Non-Interference Law"

"It must be whatever governing body handles universal-scale matters, making sure someone doesn't fiddle about with the primitives, as it were. Can it be accessed anyway, undetectably?"

"There does appear to be non-locked information regarding what will allow access. If a native resident to the planet locked is seeking access, it is to be granted. Shall I submit an inquiry to the Conclave by that rule?"

"Yeah, go ahead. Let me know when we can

get in."

"Proximity Alert."

That meant someone was at the door of the shop. The place itself was open 24 hours, with a sign on the door saying: HIT THE BELL IF THE DOOR IS LOCKED. I MIGHT BE WORKING. The proximity alert came in when someone hit said bell. Miles walked up from the basement the Techbooth was in, and remotely unlocked the door to let a middle-aged couple in to browse.

"Sorry about that, was working," Miles said.

"Don't worry about it, not like it was raining. Have you got fuel canisters here?" one of the gentlemen asked.

"I do, right over there," Miles said, pointing at some filled gas cans for emergency fueling. "Haven't exactly got pumps, but this is the next best thing. If the car's hybrid-electric, I do have a charge post as well."

"Well, in that case, I think we'd rather do that," the other said. "But I didn't see any charge post."

"That was the... the thing outside. The one you were all 'oh no, that's not a charge post! There's no way one would be all the way out here!'"

"Fine, I'll go plug it in," the younger of the two—though not by much—grumbled as he went out the door.

"It's early in the morning, isn't it?" Miles asked.

"Yeah, about 4:30. You didn't notice?"

"I was working, I usually don't notice when it comes to timekeeping." Which was only partially true. The Aura had eliminated Miles's need to sleep, and thus he was constantly awake and alert as if it were midday. The second half of the couple came back in after plugging their car to the charge post.

"Is this menu all-hours?" he asked as he looked at it.

"Not sure why else it'd be out there," Miles informed. The two nodded to each other, deciding that they were indeed hungry. Miles also couldn't help but notice that the two were looking around the ceiling and walls, where cameras normally were. They didn't seem as nervous as they did cautious. They ordered a full Irish breakfast to share, which Miles knew how to make, which would only be supplemented by The Aura's abilities. Walking into the back kitchen out of view of the rest of the building, Miles simply used The Aura to sort of "autopilot" himself as he made the full Irish, timing with when he began cooking the bangers, followed by the beans before the bacon and pudding slices. Less than fifteen minutes later, and the whole thing was done, which he promptly delivered to the two waiting in the sitting area.

Miles looked at the computer at the register he

had, that was connected to the Techbooth downstairs, and he typed an inquiry: ARE THOSE TWO IN DANGER?

Techbooth scanned their faces remotely, with cameras smaller than even some of the most trained eyes could see, and cross-referenced them with anything that might be of note. After interpreting the data, a message was displayed for Miles: THEY ARE BEING HUNTED FOR BEING TOGETHER BY A HATE GROUP.

Miles typed one more message to Techbooth: WHAT IS THE STATUS OF THEIR FOES?

A moment passed.

THEIR SEARCH PARTY IS TEN MILES AWAY, HEADING DOWN THE HIGHWAY. THEY WILL LIKELY SEE AND ENTER THIS ESTABLISHMENT.

"Shit," Miles said aloud. The two looked over to Miles, a little worried.

"They're following you two," Miles said, confirming their worry. "They're ten miles out, and will definitely come in here."

They were just about to scramble to their feet, when Miles stopped them, piping up. "If you run, you'll die tired. Stay here, and you're under my protection, and I will not fail. I know you're wondering how I know, and you also might be thinking that you'll just be thankful for the warning, regardless of how I can give it. But they're gonna catch up one way or another, because I guess that's just how petty and spiteful people are. Head up those stairs, and don't make any noise. I will deal with your enemies. I promise."

The two looked at each other, then back to Miles. "I'd ask how the hell we can trust you, but you knew they were coming. I guess we can't afford to ask questions about our blessings," the older one said, as his partner made his way up the stairs.

"Good man," Miles said. "What's your names?"

"I'm Jarrek. He's Brian."

"Jarrek's a good name, don't lose it. Now get up there."

"Are you going to kill them?"

"Hopefully. But maybe it won't come to that."

Jarrek went up the stairs along with Brian to hide, and a few minutes later, a single person walked through the door. With The Aura, Miles could tell he was concealing a pistol on his hip, but in a rather shoddy holster with no retention, like the kind one of those couch commandos who unironically would rather be able to draw their weapon half a second faster than make sure someone can't just yank it from behind would use, since they believe themselves just that observant, when they quite honestly would not be.

Miles understood this man was likely about to be humbled for this hubris. He walked around a bit, before asking who owns the other car, and why they weren't here. Casually, of course, in that 'painfully trying too hard to be subtle' sort of way. Miles stared at him in response.

"Cut the shit. I know why you and five others are here," Miles finally said. "Don't try to play stupid, or I won't even give you the chance to leave peacefully."

The man smirked. "A young lickspit like you shouldn't be stickin' his nose where it don't belong."

"This is my shop. Anything that happens here is exactly where my nose belongs. You get one warning. The same warning I give everyone else. This is me being kind."

"You think you're a badass, huh?" the man retorted as he drew his weapon and pulled the trigger. But nothing happened. Miles had used The Aura to jam the gun, rendering it completely useless. It was in this moment Miles sported what wasn't quite a shit-eating grin, but definitely the look of 'I will never get tired of being able to call them silly little guns.'

All the five friends of that man saw, was Miles dragging the corpse of their compatriot out the door, and tossing it towards them. The man's throat had been crushed by a hard blow, and he had died gasping for air.

"I'm willing to fight each of you hand-to-hand. Man to man, as it were. All at once, if you'd like. But anyone grabs a weapon, they don't get that honor. Guns are the cheat code of combat, and I will make sure you never get to use it. Fight me with the weapons the gods gave you, if you want to fight. Pull a weapon if you would rather just die."

Two of the men reached into their back pockets for firearms, and Miles used The Aura to conjure two knives in his hands and throw them into the cheater's throats. They died without incident. The three others were smart enough to take that offer, to Miles's surprise.

The first didn't even get to finish winding his wild haymaker before Miles kicked him in the solar plexus with the steel-toed workboots he wore. The other hesitated for a moment when he saw his friend go down so quickly, and Miles simply put that steel toe to his temple with a head-high roundhouse, something Miles was already quite good at, even before The Aura. The last one threw a straight jab, and Miles grabbed his forearm and broke his elbow severely, then cracking a rib with an elbow of his own. This last man staggered back, howling in pain from his broken arm. The first one, only having slightly recovered his wind, went for a groin punch, but was once again stopped with a steel toe, to his chin this time, seeing as he was bent over and that was the available target. Miles must've hit it hard, since this guy was no longer moving. The force of his head snapping back seemed to have broken a few vertebrae in his spine, and severed the cord, resulting in internal decapitation. The second was either dead or dying, since the depressed skull fracture certainly would've cut into his brain. The third still screamed at his broken arm, so Miles put him out of his misery by leaping forward and driving the bottom of his elbow into the top of his foe's head. Another depressed skull fracture and brain hemorrhage. Five dead homophobes. The world made that much better. Technically six when you count the first one.

Six less of the evildoers in this world was not something to protest. Disposing of their bodies was easy. Miles had used most of the trash pile from months back to create an Atomic Emancipation Grid generator, a sort of "Ultimate trash compactor". All matter vaporized in an instant, converted to breathable oxygenatious air. Naturally, that's where their bodies went, and their car.

Miles went back into his shop, and up the stairs to where Jarrek and Brian were waiting. "They're gone. Won't be able to bother you anymore."

Brian breathed an audible sigh of relief, and Jarrek approached Miles.

"I suppose you should avoid telling me what you did. Don't want to be an accomplice."

"Six less of that kind of person in the world? No one reasonable will miss them," Miles said. "And even if they do trace this whole ordeal, they'll trace it to me and not you. If you two know where you're going, then I advise you start getting there. And finish that breakfast of yours."

Jarrek laughed, and the two did indeed finish the breakfast in the sitting area, before leaving on their way. There was no mistake about it, Miles felt victorious. Six enemies of the world, gone. The Aura had given him the power to finally do something right. But he pondered. Could he indeed snap his fingers and all the evil people of the world would drop dead in agony? Yes. But he almost felt compelled to refrain from that, maybe at most a high-profile assassination of a corrupt politician or a greedy billionaire. Maybe just slit their throat in the night, then their beneficiaries. But Miles seemed to understand to himself that it just wouldn't really work like that. Yes, it would be right. Yes, it would be good. But it seemed that all it would do would be to make the world weaker overall. If he does all the protecting for them, how would they protect themselves?

Today was because it was the right thing to do. On that small scale, allowing a good couple to make their escape from those who hated them without cause.

It was then Miles had his epiphany. His was to make something *able* to happen, rather than to do it outright. Put the pieces right there, and let them be easily put together. He could be the catalyst that would allow the world to be saved, because if he just waved his arms around and made it all 'better,' no one would learn.

But it could be minor things, things that allow more to happen. The fascist open-carrying a rifle outside a mosque or synagogue, only allowed to do so by the literal letter or law and not its spirit, he could make that trigger finger drift just that little bit, unnoticed, and when someone finally called the police, that finger twitches and the rifle goes off. The deserved punishment is administered, and their life justly ruined.

Not making such a person trip over and break their skull open on a rock, because that's clumsy luck. But making such a person look like a complete fool, with such improper firearm discipline, that finally sparks this and that and leads to the world being better overall, not by Miles's direct action, but because Miles made it able to happen. This was how he was to act with this power of his, at least on Earth, where power like his wasn't in direct conflict with the majority understanding of reality.

But Malin did ask him to figure out that signal, and Techbooth did just alert him that new information was available. He went back into the basement for this.

"A transmission originating from Turazin is requesting communication. Turazin is the home base of the Conclave of Sentience, and The Hideout, considered the largest library-slash-information repository in the known universe."

"Patch it through, then," Miles said.

"To whomever has requested access to the Galactic Network, this is Xenidar Ralkas, leader of The Hideout. I represent the Conclave of Sentience's wishes regarding the network and its maintaining. Please identify yourself by name, species and planet of origin."

"My name is Miles Sorvenjar Radien... human... of Earth" The word human was said in a very negative tone, as if it's truth angered Miles on an existential level.

"Sounds like you're not overly fond of that," Xenidar replied, the transmission finally now showing his picture. A Vulpian, but much smaller in stature. Possibly a genetic variant Miles was unaware of. "This is honestly just standard proceeding, and I do need you to answer these questions I have truthfully before I can give your device access to the Galus-Net."

Miles nodded. "If you don't mind me asking, what species are you? I can tell you're Vulpian, but I've only met one type, likely the Cynofrax-specific ones.

"I'm a Talvas Vulpian. There's three major variants, and dozens of minor ones. The other is the Death World Vulpians. My personal home planet was Turazin here, but my species originates from Talvakorrik. The Death Worlders are from Raon-Arashal, which you'll be able to find out more if you can answer my questions now." Xenidar cleared his throat, and looked to Miles. Miles nodded again. "For what reason did you need the services of the Galus-Net?"

"I wanted to look up an energy signature's wavelength to see if it was a known type."

Xenidar nodded, in a 'fair enough' sort of way. "Are you a native of the planet you are accessing the Galus-Net on?"

"Yes."

"The location of your planet is not in the Galus-Net's database. Are you willing to designate a name for your planet and species, as well as any reason they may be considered sentient, under this definition, known as The Pillars Three?" At that, a window popped up onscreen, reading 'The Pillars Three'. It appeared to be a test for sentience, based on one's ability to recognize that they are alive, that they can die, and that at any given moment, they may or may not want to die. A solid definition, if not absolute. Miles thought for a moment, making sure he didn't rush his response.

"This planet is named Earth, and the... self-declared dominant species on it, to which I disdainfully belong is called Humans. There are many, many other species on this world as well, some likely sentient, most likely not. As for the humans, I can confirm their sentience by this definition. Techbooth, grant Xenidar access to Earth's internal communications and information networks. Although, I'm afraid you're going to have a lot of junk to sort through if you take all of that at once. I recommend designated libraries for the bulk of it. And maybe an army of strong-willed volunteers..." Miles finally said to Xenidar.

Xenidar took a look at a few things, then nodded. "Ok, yeah, you guys are definitely sentient. Tell you what, though... the Conclave would probably reject them from joining the wider universe's community. I'll file the humans as a Class 3C, a partial recognition, but large-scale communication with the species is still not allowed, due to an established unreadiness... I'll say under... immoral ideals?"

"Certainly fits," Miles remarked. "There's more reasons than that, though."

"I only need the one right now," Xenidar said as he typed on his end. "All right, Miles. I'm giving this device access to the Galus-Net. You are responsible for protecting this device from other members of your species, or granting access at your discretion."

Miles nodded.

"On a personal note, Miles, I am curious what that wavelength was you wanted to cross-reference. The Hideout is the single largest repository of information in the known united universe," Xenidar said curiously. "Of course, I only mean united as in communicable with each other... it'd be pretty fuckin' silly to have multiple galaxies under one banner..."

"Techbooth, send Xenidar the data Malin gave us."

Xenidar took a look, and then a double-take, with a rather worried expression on his face.

"Miles, are you sure these readings are accurate?" he finally asked.

"Not at all. This is data taken from a rather primitive energy scanner, and perhaps I could get schematics for a better one."

Some blueprints and material manifests showed up on Miles's screen.

"You should be able to make one of these with the materials on your planet. It's a seventh-generation energy scanner. Pretty standard issue, and connected to the Galus-Net's databases on energy types. Once you've done that, I'd appreciate if you'd let me know the reading, because I hope this one you've sent me isn't entirely accurate."

"We'll worry about it when we do, I suppose. I'll get on it. Thanks, Xenidar."

"Welcome to the universe, Miles Radien."

Xenidar's transmission switched off, and Techbooth was back to its desktop of sorts, awaiting the next input, which took Miles a moment to figure out.

"Tell you what, using Xenidar's schematics for that energy scanner, find out what tools and what materials we need to make it here on Earth, and how much that might cost. Draft me up at least five options, sorted by, say... priority on which one will have the most use in creating higher technology further down the line."

Techbooth made its confirmation noise before getting to work, anticipating a few minutes before the calculations were done. After all, it had the entirety of Earth's knowledge to sift through, both true and false. The doorbell of the shop rang again.

CHAPTER THE FIFTH

Miles walked up and saw an unfamiliar woman at the door, alone. He unlocked the door remotely and let her in. Although she did seem a bit off, more in just the execution of being a person, which was a bit of a tip.

"Veralis, if that's you, then that's a pretty sad attempt at subtlety," Miles said cautiously, to which the woman nodded, then a blue mist surrounded her, and Veralis stood in her place.

"It was worth a try," Veralis said. "Anything to report, or tell me, or whatever?"

Miles recounted the story of Malin and ETAL-RARC, as well as what he had been doing personally over the time he spent back on Earth, even that little epiphany of his. Veralis seemed particularly intrigued at that.

"That's... an interesting way to put it. I knew there was more to you when you were granted The Aura, I've always known it, honestly. I've just never been sure what, exactly. I've got a few theories, but I don't want to be wrong, so I'll just keep them to myself until they get shown to be one way or the other."

Miles nodded understandingly. He didn't want to get oversold on something he would turn out not to be. Besides, the idea of fated roles didn't particularly appeal to him.

"But this Malin, and ETAL-RARC... it's a lot more wisdom than what you've told me the humans are like. But I did take the time to look at some of their history... no wonder you hate them. And honestly, that phrase you told me of 'A person is smart, but people are dumb, panicky animals' makes a hell of a lot more sense now. I can definitely think of single humans that could be trusted as part of the wider universe, but the whole species? Gods, not a chance. What a conflicting bunch, your kinsmen."

"Yeah..." Miles partially lamented. "On the one hand, I don't think the universe would miss them if they all up and died. On the other, they've had some good ideas."

"They've had you."

"Oh, don't give them credit for that."

The two laughed. Miles got a ping from the computer on the shop floor, and led Veralis down into the basement with Techbooth.

"Ok, Techbooth, what have you figured?"

"Utilizing Galus-Net data and material availability, I've created a list of tools you could create or otherwise acquire to have a fully-functional planetary base, as per the guide mentioned in Flora Valtarius's 'Best Practices of Planetary Base Building and Equipping' manual."

The screen then flashed with a list of things the base should be capable of doing, and the tools needed to fulfill that role.

MAIN PLANETARY BASE, PERSONAL-SCALE

o SUSTENANCE MANUFACTURING AND PROCESSING CABABILITIES (ALREADY PRESENT, DESIGNATION "KITCHEN")

o POINT AND AREA DEFENSE (RECOMMEND AUTO-TURRETS, KINETIC PROJECTILE GIVEN LOCAL TECHNOLOGY)

o TOOL FABRICATION CAPABILITY (RECOMMEND ATOMIC FORGE, CAN BE CREATED WITH EARTH MATERIALS, BUT THE DEVICE WILL BE RATHER BULKY, ABOUT THE SIZE OF THE AVERAGE EARTH CAR)

o PERSONAL DEFENSE CAPABILITY (RECOMMEND

RIFLE, SIDEARM, MELEE INSTRUMENT GIVEN USER BIOLOGY)

- o   PERSONAL FITNESS AND TRAINING EQUIPMENT (RECOMMEND HOLOGRAPHIC ARENA)

"Well, I might just have my work cut out for me," Miles said.

"I can get you those things so you don't have to make Earth-based knockoffs. Especially if it's only you using them," Veralis mentioned.

"Well, then that would be wonderful," Miles said, breathing a sigh of relief.

"Now then, you should probably come with me in regards for personal weapons. Tailoring to the user, and all."

Miles nodded, and Veralis extended her arm, Miles taking it. The two suddenly found themselves in a sort of desert town, definitely on a different planet. One could only say 'sort of desert town,' as while the surrounding landscape was indeed sandy dunes and howling winds, the civilization itself clearly used higher technology to protect itself from incurring hostile elements, as if the desert blew around a force field, which was honestly likely the case.

Veralis went up to a vendor at what was likely a market they were standing in, and spoke to... her. Miles seemed to inherently understand what species and gender everyone around him was, likely a facet of The Aura's gifts. Her indeed, of the Taigron species, appearing to be bipedal tigers. He was starting to like this universe if it were full of creatures like this. Then again, it was most likely that anthropomorphic-based evolution was just a natural advantage in most environments.

"Miles Radien, follow me please," The Taigron asked of him, and Miles followed. He was soon looking at a massive underground armory and training grounds. "Stand in that scanner?" So he did.

"It's just taking a basic body profile, figuring out what weapons and weight actually make sense for you, biologically speaking. It'd be pretty dumb to hand you a Kendrosian Volkaskral. You need four arms for those," Veralis explained.

Miles didn't even bother asking what the hell a Volkaskral even looked like. The Taigron spoke next.

"Miles, could you uh... describe your melee combat tactics? What kind of weapons do you like up close?" she asked.

"I trained in Eskrima, a martial art from my world. It uh... heavily emphasizes mobility, agility, precision and speed of movement. One of the big tactics is to hit someone's hand with a stick. Of course, the idea behind it is that anything you can do with a stick, you can do with a sword, knife, your empty hands, even a spear or staff. A stick or sword is basically an extension of your arm, and a knife... well, that's just more making the reach of your fingertips pointy."

"Something like this, maybe?" A 3D hologram showed up in front of Miles.

"Well, that's just a Cutlass. I've always liked fighting with those."

Veralis nodded. "All the fixings. Novasteel, Hunderfold, the whole thing." The armsmaster wrote that down, clearly understanding what that meant, unlike Miles.

"As for ranged weapons? If you could have any kind of ranged weapon, what would it be? And I don't mean just names of weapon models, I mean, what would that weapon do?" the armsmaster continued.

"Well, I'd like a rifle to be able to switch between long-range sniping and short-range urban battle. I'd definitely want something that can fit in an ankle holster as well, in case it got that bad."

"Well, that makes you easier to arm than most," the armsmaster commented, seemingly relieved. "What do you think, Veralis? For the rifle, probably a Talvakorrik Battle Rifle?"

"No, he wanted configurable for multiple ranges, not just compatible. Orvitarian Collapse Rifle for sure.

But definitely a Talvakorrik AZP-621 for his hip or ankle. As for armor… I'd say something that can take the form of his regular clothes. Maybe… Salnweave garments?"

The armsmaster continued with her notes as Veralis placed the order.

"I do have The Aura, you know," Miles said, noting that armored clothes might not be necessary given his enhanced bodily healing ability. Veralis thought for a moment, then nodded and signaled for the armsmaster to cancel that.

"Defense grid generator for sure, though. One of the Hajivakk ones. Also, one of those detector module glasses, either Redarian or Cynofraxian, whichever generation's currently got the better functionality."

"I think the Cynofrax one's got the edge right now. All tailored, I assume?"

"Aye, all tailored. Scan done?"

The armsmaster looked at a screen, nodded, then motioned for Miles to step down. "We'll have them in two weeks, tops." Veralis nodded back to her, and offered her arm again to Miles, and they teleported back to Earth, at the Fourteen Werewolves.

"Well, that was quick," Miles commented.

"Quick, and very necessary. I'll get ahold of those tools, and I think I know just which ones would work for you."

Miles nodded, and Veralis teleported off. A few seconds later, a big sigh from Miles. "Hell of a day, and it's only really just started."

He looked at the clock. It wasn't too long ago that he wished Jarrek and Brian well on their journey.

"I suppose my definition of a day is gonna change with this no-need-to-sleep deal. Definitely not complaining, though."

CHAPTER THE SIXTH

Miles sat at a table in the basement of his shop, having a proper moment of his own for the first time in a while. Between the customers he had, and the help he was giving to those who needed it, he had been rather occupied for the past while, but now he had a moment, closing his eyes and hearing the hum of silence, soon bringing into his vision an effigy of some kind, a sort of 'advanced imaginary friend' that he'd just talk to and give updates, and say how he felt about them. He hadn't summoned the effigy for a while, but now he had some time to talk to his vision of 'himself but stronger'.

"It's been a while, hasn't it?" Miles started, to no response. The effigy never responded. He never needed to. "But this is definitely something. I... all the worlds.

The worlds in my head. I can live out those silly dreams, that I guess aren't so silly anymore. A new friend of mine, Veralis, she's been getting me the tools to make this base properly mine. And I've got that shop now! Remember that shop with that utter trash name I dreamed of having? I got it, we're in the basement now!"

Miles was interrupted by Techbooth informing him that the energy scanner had finished it's "Scan-Pulse" of the entire planet. It had only taken a while because Miles had told it to do an exceptionally detailed scan, really seeing what was up on this planet. "We'll talk more later." He quickly closed his eyes, 'dismissing' the effigy, before looking at the screen to see what the scan revealed.

THREE DOMINANT ENERGIES DETECTED
DEMONIC, SUBTYPE "DECEIVER DEMON"
DEMONIC, DARK SIX
AURA UNAREL CYNFRAXA

Miles figured that "Aura Unarel Cynfraxa" meant The Aura, likely in the language it was first described in. He seemed to understand, through that power, that it essentially meant "The power to make all the worlds safe", though the more literal translation of the precursor language was more "Power, World, People's Haven", at least word-for-word. The message was there, though, and that probably was the full proper name of

The Aura. But Demonic? Is that what Xenidar was doing a double-take on?

Miles had Techbooth contact Xenidar again, and he quickly answered.

"I've made a proper scanner, and here's the readings."

Xenidar took a look at them, and sighed. "Yeah, I was worried about that. Basically, you've got a literal Demon on your planet. A proper Demon from actual Hell. Specifically, a Deceiver Demon. Infiltrationist of the Burning Hells, and... they've got a following."

Miles was rather confused by this information. "Am I about to find out about and get pulled into a war that's been going on for a hell of a lot longer than most people have a number for?"

"Yes, and no," Xenidar explained. "I'm sure you've figured there weren't always barriers between realms of creation. This was known as the Time of Demons, or some call it the War For Reality. At least, they did, until nowadays, its started to be accepted as the First War For Reality. It was... billions of years ago, and The Aura Prism was made for the purpose of creating and maintaining barriers between reality, and Hell itself, and their masters, the Dark Six. They are the lords of evil, and every depiction of the devil your species might have. I'm looking at your planet's mythologies right now, and first let me say that the... Norsemen? Orcadian? That general area. Yeah, they've got some bangers. Nuckelavee? Basically a Psychosia Demon. Different names for the same creatures and concepts. But anyways, Earth's currently playing host to a Deceiver Demon, and they've been there a long time from the looks of it, gradually implanting themselves in the very culture of the species, practically weaving Demonic energy into the DNA of the race itself. A very slow burn, slow enough that the rest of the universe wouldn't notice. But it's also slow enough that it's not too late for your kin."

Miles immediately pointed the scanner at himself, configuring it to search for the Demonic energy. It turned up negative.

"Like I said, not too late for your kin," Xenidar continued. "And also like I said, *practically* weaving Demonic energy into human DNA. They clearly haven't succeeded yet."

"So, what can or should be done? I'm admittedly new to this whole power-wielding deal, and only just found out that Demons are a proper thing, and existential threat," Miles asked.

"Honestly? The best course of action is to just lay low and help out where you can, at least until something more permanent gets figured out. If Earth does attract outside attention, though, it's possible the planet might be destroyed if ruled corrupted. And it might not even be an authorized strike, there are plenty who don't care to take the chance, and the worst part is that they're not entirely wrong to operate like that."

Miles thought for a moment. "I'll do just that. Help out where I can, and make it at least plausible that I don't have cosmic powers at my back to make it happen. Hopefully, something will figure itself out from there just from the process of progress."

Xenidar nodded, and switched off his transmission. The door rang again. Some serious timing, Miles thought as he walked upstairs, then immediately sealed off the basement when he saw Malin walk through the door.

"You're really not easy to find," Malin commented.

"I don't like being followed," Miles asserted. "I believe I made that clear last time."

"Well, I hope you've got something for me in regards to that energy."

"Bold of you to assume I'm just going to tell you after I believe you agreed to stop fuckin' following me."

Malin sighed. "Is this the conversation we're going to have? Now? How much of the Earth is at stake, and how petty are you willing to be about it?"

"That's something that right now, only I know. And even then, I'm willing to be just as perceptively petty as you want to lie to yourself about it. I told you I'd give you an answer when I could get it, and no sooner. You're lucky, because I do have the answer, and you've got good timing. You're also unlucky because right now I feel no obligation to give it to you after you breached our agreement to not. Follow. Me."

"How much is at stake from that... energy?"

"All of the universe is at stake. Every planet orbiting every star, and every being on all of them are in danger from this energy. And if I showed this to them, that Earth had that energy, they'd know just how much danger they're in, and they'll not be taking any chances. Yes, that means they're going to blow the Earth to dust. So if all reality is at stake, who's gonna lose sleep over one backwater planet populated exclusively by spiteful, ever-so corruptible manifests of the kind of petty drama that kills so many? The answer is not me."

Malin stood there, silent, but not stunned.

"Don't. Follow. Me," Miles reiterated. "Now then, I'm gonna tell you what exactly this energy is, with the understanding that if you breach this agreement again, I *will* give this information also to the nearest passing ship with a planet-killing weapon to let them decide what to do about it. They might spare you, they might not. Follow me again, and you'll be taking that chance."

A moment passed before Miles spoke again. There were a lot of things Malin could say, but what good would it do?

"What you picked up, wherever it is you did, it's Demonic. And yes, I mean literal Demons from literal Hell. Whichever image you've got in your head about what that looks like, it's there, along with everyone else's perceptions of it when they hear the word. Their masters, the ones who create this energy that leaves this trace, are called the Dark Six. They're the lords of evil, or whatever you wanna call them to prove the point. They're the big bad of the universe, a threat from outside it, coming in to conquer. So my question is, where did this signature originate?"

"From a single person." Malin sighed, and put a file folder on the counter Miles was behind. "It wasn't easy to confirm, either. And I think you can see why."

The dossier contained information about a single person, a well-known animator and children's cartoon creator. It appeared to be that she had been using her creations to turn individuals to servitude towards the Dark Six, by lacing the very transmissions that aired the shows with Demonic energy. DVDs of the show, digital downloads, all of them containing just that faintest of traces, enough to exist and be binding.

As it turned out, an estimated eight million people on the planet, likely more, were already Demonic servants. Humans who had their consciousness swapped with a Demon's, as if remotely controlled all the way from Hell. The process, it seemed, was that all a person had to do was make a verbal declaration of servitude. To say with intent, that they are allying themselves with the Dark Six. But the Deceiver Demon, as Xenidar called it, was clearly clever, lacing Demonic energy into her creations meant that if you so much as declared yourself allied to the *creation*, it was close enough, and now they had you. But only one of the shows she created had this energy present, likely a ploy to build up her reputation with genuinely harmless creations, and to begin the conversion once everyone's complacent and accepting of her work. Miles made this clear as he explained to her these findings of his.

"The link is her," Malin said. "We've even figured out that if she dies, the link is severed. All those people lose that energy trace. And from what you tell me, the Demons in their heads are gone."

"Yes," Miles said, rubbing his head as if he were about to deliver some bad news. "The problem is that I don't know what's going to happen to the people. One possibility is that they're just gonna get themselves back. However, the more likely outcomes are that they get themselves back, but in the state they were in just before they were converted. This means that people who had been servants of the Dark Six for their entire lives are going to regress back to that... five-year old state they were in when they said they liked the show. It's also possible that all those people will drop dead."

"My god," Malin muttered, genuinely surprised and pained at this knowledge. "This... Demon, has to die. But when it does, up to ten million people drop dead or regress, some maybe only months, but others... possibly a whole lifetime."

"That's likely what that Deceiver is counting on," Miles said. "It's integrated itself so well and so perfectly into the human race, that even if people know what she looks like without what's likely a morphic illusion, they get tripped up on the consequences. Maybe they try to find another way, but all that time, one thing is happening: The Demon isn't being stopped."

Malin assured that ETAL-RARC would try to come up with a plan, and following the understanding that Miles would be working on and executing his own, left. Thus, Miles had only himself and his thoughts to attend to. Soon, those thoughts came up with that plan of his.

The Deceiver's identity may have been known to Miles and ETAL-RARC, but not the rest of the human race. There was also no way to convince the peoples of

Earth that a beloved animator was a Demon taken human form. They had to be shown. Upon the Deceiver's death, the human race would make its greatest discovery: They are not alone. So far from alone.

Miles figured that there had to be a way to force the Demon out of morphic illusion, and reveal its true form. A few searches on Turazin's database later, and Miles had his answer: Counter-Catalystic Energy. For all forms of power in the universe, there existed a Counter-Catalyst for it. The opposite of the power's frequency, as it were. But it was a lot more complicated as a process than that. But there was a known Counter-Catalyst for Demonic energy. If Miles could expose the Demon to the energy, they would be forced to revert to their true form in order to resist the anti-power, or risk a Malign Transformation due to the conflicting powers present. They would die painfully, and become a twisted hybrid of the two forms they tried to hold. Fortunately, this anti-power could be contained as a solid crystal. It would take months for the Atomic Forge that he had made from plans he found on the Galus-Net, but it was something. Miles uploaded the schematic for the Counter-Catalyst to the Forge, and pressed the green button on it.

ESTIMATED TIME TO COMPLETION

106 DAYS

"Sounds about right," Miles remarked.

CHAPTER THE SEVENTH

Unil Givalien, ken unil val seyn valn
Unil Giraydien, ken unil rel seyn raydn
Unil Gidokien, ken unil gishal seyn Dokn
Unil Gikalsien, ken unil zholl seyn zholln
Aldka Sehlkavhika, þsehlkoska
Aldka Sehlhaldn, þlurein
Aldka Sehlflown, aldka Sehlakarka
Gidaan taydeltn aravinda Giraydien

Miles woke up from his bed. But The Aura made it so that he didn't need to sleep... right?

He walked outside the small shed acting as a bedroom next to the Fourteen Werewolves, but something seemed off about the world. Soon, he figured it out. Everything had stopped. The wind, the grass, nothing moved except him. A vision, perhaps? A side effect of his power? An attack?

"What do you know, Miles Radien?" a voice asked of him. Not booming, not wispy, but still just as everywhere, like it was being spoken in his mind, like one's own thoughts.

"Right now, not much," Miles replied to the air. "This is a vision? A dream? The Aura should've fixed that whole sleep thing!"

"This is no dream, you could call it a vision. You're still in reality, the universe you've always stood in. Time simply is moving far slower for you. You perceive a moment, so quickly that the rest of creation simply cannot... catch up, as it were."

"If this is still reality, then why does the sky look like I clipped outside the map?" And the sky was truly wrong, in that surreal regard. Like you had flown outside of a video game's 3D environment through cheats, seeing the light source as it becomes the rest of the void you look around, resetting when you turn back towards the game's space proper.

"It's a form you understand," this strange voice said, but certainly didn't clarify. "You're of a different kind now, who wields The Aura. But even this name isn't its only one. It is however, the name you understand. One calls it The Aura, and you know what that means. An ever-present power existing at all points in space and time. It always was there, it always is there, it always will be there. Even some humans have different names for it. Some said Dark Energy, but you know Dark Energy to be something else."

Miles waited for the next part of the explanation.

"You might know Dark Energy as the energy present even in truly empty space, not even occupied by neutrinos and other... non-interactive matter. But that is not The Aura. The sky does not look as it does right now, but it is a form you can understand the message of: A different instance of reality, wherein time has slowed to such that crawl, almost as if it's stopped. The message stands, regardless of the words or sights it wraps itself in."

"I suppose that's how the Universal Understanding that the Prism talked about works? My own little idiolect is now what I hear when anyone speaks? The message gets delivered in the way it would need to be for me to understand?"

"Correct." It was only now that Miles realized he had been walking down the highway away from his traveler's stop.

"You're not even the Prism, are you?" Miles finally asked.

"No. But what do you know, Miles Radien?"

Like this voice said, Miles understood what that meant. He knew what the answer was, even as vague as this question's words alone were.

"I stand alone," he answered. "Radien stands alone. But that's okay. It's better that way."

"You do know that," the voice stated. Not exactly an agreement or a questioning, but an acknowledgment of what Miles knew of himself, and of his existence.

"So why are you speaking to me, whoever you even are? And what are these words that I can almost see in my head? Unil Givalien... what even is that? Universal Understanding clearly isn't if I don't know what that's supposed to mean."

A few moments passed.

"Unless I do know. I just... don't have the words that describe them. Those words are of such grander scale than the ones that exist in the language I grew up speaking. So much more... iron, and resolute. I can't seem to find the word for it, and I'm almost tempted to make one up."

"All languages are made up. Messages, as a phenomenon, as a thing to be given and received can be altered as needed for any of them. Universal Understanding, or I suppose a better term might be Universal Linguistics allows all those messages to be known and understood by whoever holds it, without the inherent problems of a completely different word for the same concept, whatever reason that might be."

"But I must ask... who are you?" Miles remembered to question. "Who even speaks to me like I might in my own head, with that sort of personal intuition?"

"The Aura."

Miles found himself back in the bed again. No time had passed between Malin leaving The Fourteen Werewolves and Miles beginning the construction of his Counter-Catalyst, and now as he sat and soon stood up. He rubbed his face, and groaned slightly.

"A whole new understanding of reality is going to take some getting used to."

People came in and out of the traveler's stop a couple times a day, this waystation being along the highway itself. It was good fun for Miles to have this sort of flow to his day, running his business comfortably. He wasn't making much profit from it, if at all. But that leftover trash he had from building both the Fourteen Werewolves and his little pseudo-house he had rearranged its atoms to gold. So money really wasn't going to be an issue for him. He did, after some time and questions asked within, put up a sign inside the store itself reading "If you need to ask, you're not prepared to know."

"I'm such trash," he said to himself as he mounted the sign. Veralis then walked through the door.

"It is certainly a name to be reckoned with," she said. Miles already knew she was there, though.

"Well, like I said, I'm rather trash. Did you need something?"

The two went down to the basement with Techbooth, and Veralis began to place a couple of small circular devices on the ground. Once she was done, a workshop's worth of tools materialized in, the kind that would make any science fiction fan quite possibly orgasm on the spot.

"It wasn't easy, but I managed to get a Keystone Forge with all the fixings. This whole setup is that. I believe you used common trash to construct this place, utilizing rapid atomic fission-fusion via The Aura, correct? Like the Atomic Forge making your counter-catalyst?"

Miles nodded. Veralis seemed impressed that the idea had to him so quickly.

"Keystone Forge basically does that with a lot less personal power, hooking directly to that central catalyst right there... and that's an impressive one for your first try. It'll work excellently. Build area is right here, and a matter projector to assemble it. Makes constructing turrets or small vehicles way easier." She then produced some chalk in her hand... or paw, rather, and drew a large square on the empty ground. "Atomic emancipator to deconstruct trash or… bodies, given the incident you told me about. This one's way more efficient than yours right now. It'll store the raw protons and neutrons for fusion, recycling most of the energy produced by the fission, and in an emergency, it can convert to raw power immediately. Biological matter tends to give more power, like plants and such. Or bodies. I already mentioned bodies, didn't I?"

She looked back at Miles with that, and he nodded in a sort of 'You did, but in a different context.' way.

"Basically, this setup you've got here now will do whatever you need it to. Oh! And I almost forgot…"

Veralis placed another device on the ground, and some kind of projector unit warped in. "Just find a large, empty, enclosed space for this. That's your Holographic Arena projector. For training. And those weapons from Orvitaire are… here."

Another device and warp-in later, and a large case was shown to Miles. "Orvitaire? That's where we were?" he asked.

"Yes. Orvitaire, sometimes referred to as The Martial Planet. You might enjoy it on a proper trip. And The Aura Runner, which has been on Cynofrax yet for a while, has been approved to be in your possession now.

It was being held until the identity of the Draconian who died could be proved legitimate in ownership... It's a process. Point is, The Aura Runner is yours now," Veralis explained, then handed Miles an amber-colored triangular gadget. "Here's the Chronokey and Recall."

"Thanks, Veralis," Miles said. Not slowly, and certainly not confused, but... as if still taking it all in. Veralis nodded, and prepared to head out.

"I know it's a lot at first. But you'll figure it out. I trust you to do that."

Miles looked up at her, shocked. He could hardly believe someone just casually said that to him. "You... do?"

Veralis seemed confused at first, but then realized just what she had told him. "Oh, gods... I'm so sorry. And you know why." She extended an arm to him. Miles took it, just holding for a bit. He looked up, his breathing almost more along the lines of short sighs.

"The tech isn't the hard part. It's seeing such casual truth after all my time. Such inherent trust and understanding... I don't know how to react." He took a deep breath in and out, and let go of Veralis's arm. "I'll control myself. I'll keep my head in the game on this. But thank you. Really."

Veralis nodded, and headed off, soon warping back to Cynofrax, to her home. She was so appalled that this was Miles's experience of life. Not at Miles, but at his life, and the people who made it that way. "A person is smart, indeed."

Miles did quickly regain his composure, and checked out his weapons from Orvitaire. A long rifle, with what looked to be a hell of a scope on it. He took the surprisingly light instrument in his hands, and looked through the scope, before quickly putting it back down, deciding he needed a proper testing range.

A few hours later, and Miles had done his personal technique to make buildings and had excavated an underground bunker, about the size of two shipping containers attached to the Fourteen Werewolves, with its own power generator. He placed the projector down, and pushed the central power button. It scanned the room, and displayed a menu of things to do.

"Let's do a weapons test, long-range."

The rifle showed itself to be just what it was called, an Orvitarian Collapse Rifle. With the flick of a switch, it transformed from a sniper's tool to a close quarters battle rifle, the sort of 'stubby' kind you'd take into an urban environment. The AZP-621 was actually more a two-handed pistol, but was able to take any magazine from any weapon, and fire any bullets. A Morphic Metal magazine catch and barrel made it able to adapt to munition types. As for his cutlass, the blade shone in a brilliant flow of colors across a material folded at least... well, Miles couldn't actually tell how many folds there were, but there had to be a lot. He then recalled Veralis's material specification back on Orvitaire, realizing he was looking at Novasteel. The Holographic Arena spawned him targets, static and mobile, and even fighting. This was where he could train himself, like Veralis said.

With now the days' training done, all that was left was to keep training, keep being a general help around the place, and wait for that Counter-Catalyst to finish. He had a new guitar now, and figured now might be a decent time to play a bit, while something new and exciting prepared to show itself. An old original of his to start off, and get back in the loop of playing, one he called "The Ballad of Karma's Fall".

Miles put down his guitar after that, and pondered. Did that song mean anything now? He had his power, and he could have his worlds to see and experience. There would have been more questions if someone didn't walk through the door to The Fourteen Werewolves. It was none other than Jarrek.

"I never got to thank you proper for your help," he said.

"It's fine. Your survival was reward enough," Miles assured. "I'm Miles Radien, by the way. Radien works too."

A few moments of silence passed, as if they both understood already this meeting. No more words to describe it, but they just both knew well that there was no more need to talk about it. It was resolved, with hardly anything more.

"Do well by the world, Jarrek…"

"Wöllschlager," Jarrek finished, and Miles nodded. Something about him made Miles understand that there was more to him. A similar sort of non-belonging to the species and world he was born to. Jarrek took his leave, and Veralis soon followed in entrance.

"Was that a Redarian in human form?" she asked, after a quick double-take on him.

"Was it?!" Miles exclaimed. "He certainly didn't feel like he was supposed to be human!"

"Yeah, that guy was totally a Redarian. What did he say his name was?"

"Jarrek Wöllschlager." To which Veralis nodded her head in an 'of course' manner, as if she had just figured something big out.

"That… actually makes sense. He faked his death again a couple of months ago back on Redaria Prime. He's the Arch-Militant of the planet's Space Fleets. He does this usually once every two years or so, when he needs a break."

"Wait, so his people know where he is?"

"No, only that he faked his death again. Basically, Jarrek is so valuable to the Redarian Battlefleets, that he only ever gets time off if he's dead. So he just... artificially dies, as it were. The Militarium just lets him take that time he needs, because it's way better than a total burnout leading to actual death. He and his partner Brian Kandor, should be back on Redaria Prime in a couple days by now."

She paused for a moment. "Earth, though... makes sense. No one would look for him here. What was he doing here?"

"He, uh... I saved him and Brian from a group of assholes trying to kill them, who followed them here a couple of days ago. He was thanking me for killing them instead."

Veralis laughed. "Trust me, he didn't need you for it. But it's a way better cover that you did. He likely sensed a power-wielder along the highway, then hoped you'd be willing to help him so he didn't have to tear those guys to shreds himself."

Miles thought about that for a second. "Fair enough, I suppose," he concluded. "I wonder if he even goaded them into following him so he could lure them to a quiet place and dispatch them. A power-wielder would've just been an added bonus."

"It would admittedly be a Jarrek thing to do," Veralis noted. "I've little doubt you'll be seeing him again, and probably not even on Earth. But that's not why I'm here."

Veralis explained in the basement that some off-world parties had gotten word of Miles's existence. A human from a previously unacknowledged world carrying immense cosmic power. The incident with Melaqros had reached the stars, and the stars were getting curious about this Earth. Naturally, long-range scan pulses had been done on the planet, noticing the Dark Six energy. Apparently, Veralis had to explain to the Conclave of Sentience that the planet was being monitored and protected by a native now wielding The Aura, and with zero intent on letting the Demons win.

"The problem is that the Conclave isn't convinced yet," Veralis explained. "They want you to testify on Turazin, as soon as possible."

"Is there a procedure of sorts?" Miles asked.

"Answer all questions with factual truth, that's about it. They are pretty good at knowing when someone's lying intentionally. I do have to qualify the intentionally part, since they do also know pretty well when someone just didn't know that given information was incorrect."

She took a deep breath in, and calmed herself down. She wasn't nervous, just processing a lot at once.

"Whatever they ask you, just answer to the best of your knowledge on what is true." Veralis held her arm out. "Ready?"

CHAPTER THE EIGHTH

This planet of Turazin, that the Conclave was based on, wasn't much when it came to landscape. Red sandstone plains as far as the eye could see, single buildings dominating their corners of the world.

"That one's The Hideout. It's the home of the Grand Database, the biggest repository of information in the universe," Veralis explained.

"Yeah, I spoke with Xenidar a while back when I tried to access the Galus-Net. Did he…"

"No, he didn't tell the Conclave, someone else did. As the caretaker of The Hideout, Xenidar is responsible for the confidentiality of all the information he receives there. He's never required to inherently tell someone if he finds it out, but if someone asks, he usually is obligated to reveal, except in certain situations that he holds a strict personal guideline for."

"I assume that second building is for the Conclave?" Miles asked, looking over to what looked to be a silver spear of a building, to pierce the sky.

"Correct. But the actual chambers are underground, that's just there so people can see it from a distance. No one needs that big of a building to hold a single meeting. Well, at least not that tall."

Miles and Veralis made their way to the Conclave's building, and an elevator awaiting them delivered them to what was marked as "Chamber of Testament". Miles did make a comment about the theatrics of the setup, and Veralis was quick to agree, even if only because that system was what worked.

Miles entered the chamber, but it was more like a table with a single chair, and a wall in front of it. Veralis motioned for him to sit, and the wall lifted itself and showed a multitude of species and members thereof, likely representatives.

"Miles Sorvenjar Radien?" one of them, a Taigron asked.

"Aye. But you can just call me Radien if you wish."

"Excellent. Let's not waste time, then. You know just as well as us that Earth has Dark Six energy present, correct?"

"Correct. My information concludes that a Deceiver Demon has used the cover of an animated entertainment creator to transmit Dark Six energy directly towards human beholders of child-centered media, which admittedly collects more adult followers than the former, to my disdain."

Everyone at the table started taking notes. This may have been new information to some. "I estimate between six and ten million humans are affected, possibly more. If the Deceiver is killed, however, this connection will be broken, and the humans under Demonic control will be either released, or just drop dead."

"Drop dead?" a Loriken asked. The dark-furred Lupine species certainly had its share of fitness gurus, it seemed. "Six to ten million?"

"It's honestly either that or the other seven to eight billion humans, and the hundreds of billions of other species on that world. Besides, that's only one of the possible outcomes. The other is for the connection to just snap, and the slaves become free. Either way, Earth is gonna have its work cut out for them, but if we trip up on all that, that's time the Deceiver has to convert more, and amass an army."

Several of these delegates seemed rather annoyed. Not at Miles's information, but its correctness.

"I know what you're thinking, because I've thought it too. Blow it all up? The humans are one species on a planet of billions. Something to just wipe the humans alone out? The buggers have ingrained themselves on their world harder than most cancers. It's set up to burn all the same if they all fall over. There's no easy way to do this, because the actions that would be best? They still affect in some way millions. I don't like it. I hate it. I hate it, and I hate the humans, and every moment of my life I've spent as one, among them."

"Veralis Stratenheim has made clear to us your well-earned disdain for your people, and why you hold it. With the Deceiver gone, the humans will likely be thrown into massive, divisive debate of whether it was anyone's call to make, to do what did truly need be done," a Talvas Vulpian commented. "It's quite possible even, that this is a part of the human psyche owed to the Demon's work. Integrating an inherent conflict generation mechanism. It sounds like a Dark Six thing to do."

Miles nodded. "Likely. But regardless, I'll make this call, and the preparations needed for it. I'd rather not have the planet imposed upon by anyone, Conclave or otherwise. That said, if I do fail, either by corruption or death, the Conclave has my personal permission to tear Earth to atoms. I understand the risks of everything I'm doing, and planning to. I also accept what would need to be done, should I fail. I hope the rest of you trust me to know that, and act on it as per what I have wished."

"You've shown wisdom beyond what has been described of your species by Veralis, and likely yourself," a Redarian added. The people of Redaria Prime, akin to Red Pandas of Earth. Miles's theory from Orvitaire of anthropomorphic evolution being generally favorable in the universe certainly wasn't being proven wrong.

"The Conclave will entrust Earth's protection to you, Radien. Is there anything else we should know?" the Redarian continued.

"I can't guarantee my kinsmens' actions, I'm far from their leader. Individual humans are responsible themselves for whatever they do. And honestly, I don't care if the humans bite it. The universe won't miss them. But that said, they should at least get the chance to prove themselves." The Loriken nodded as soon as Miles mentioned proving oneself. "But don't act surprised if they spit on the hand that offers to them, and don't ever feel bad about punishing that person equally for it. They may be brats, but they're not literal infants."

It wasn't long after, that the Conclave agreed to leave Miles to his own devices regarding Earth, and what to do about it. So Miles headed back to Earth, and looked at the Counter-Catalyst's remaining construction time.

Until then, Miles prepared. He trained with his

weapons, and learned more of his power. He helped out where he could, for those who needed it. A hate group's members suddenly gone missing here. A mysterious cache of money for a heavily indebted person there. Recording a message for whatever happens after the Deceiver is destroyed. Miles did very much plan to make a plea to the human race to be better when he gave them their chance. He had no expectations that they would actually do it, but at least it couldn't be said that they didn't have a chance. And there would be no pity for deliberate darkness.

Eventually, that counter-catalyst was ready. But Miles had been needing to force his hand more heavily by then. This Deceiver had gotten bolder, likely upon realizing the threat Miles posed. The few dozen thugs that had been sent over the months were to show for it, and the worsening of the world around him, as if it were a ploy to bait him out, and make himself vulnerable as he tried to save someone. But now Miles had his weapon, his end all to this Demon. What he had to do now, was expose the Deceiver to the counter-catalyst's energy, and force it into its true form, and publicly. The world would now know the players in this long game of reality against Demons. And gods willing, they'd make something good of it.

One last phone call to Malin, though, to tie up

that loose end of ETAL-RARC.

"What do you have?" Malin asked.

"A plan to destroy the Deceiver. I need to know where it's assumed identity is, and I'll handle the rest."

"Edinburgh, at an animator's convention. She's the guest of honor. I can get you in, and a spot at the guest of honor dinner right next to her. What's your plan?"

"I have a device to force the Demon out of human form, and I'm going to make sure the cameras are on her when it happens. The world would never believe anything else. I can't just make her disappear, I can't do anything else than this. The world's gonna find out now, just how very not alone it is."

Malin sighed heavily. "This day was sure to come. I was just hoping I wouldn't be in charge during it. You'll need your own way to Edinburgh, but I'll bet that's easy for you."

And as soon as Miles hung up, he was there with a teleport of his own. The convention's opening ceremony wasn't for another two days, and Malin had covered his registration, dinner ticket and seating. Edinburgh for two days didn't sound bad, and Miles had been working for a while on a holographic AI to run the Fourteen Werewolves while he was out.

The two days went without incident, and finally it

was time. The opening speeches and introducing the guest of honor. But Miles had a plan that Malin didn't know about. During the two days off in Edinburgh, he'd used Techbooth to hack into the con chair's access to programming, particularly the slides and cues of the opening ceremony, planting himself to be introduced to present a gift for the illustrious animator for her contributions.

"And this last minute, most generous donation has allowed us to recognize here at these opening ceremonies, a gift to be presented to our guest of honor. Please welcome to the stage Miles Radien!"

The audience applauded as expected while Miles walked onstage, with an ornamental jewelry box in hand.

"It is my honor, ma'am, to present you this token of your contributions to animation, and our world as a whole. It's no secret your avocation to progress, and it is my honor to gift you this," Miles said, putting on a decent show, actually. The Deceiver may have been suspicious, but there wasn't anything she could do in front of all these people. Miles had her now. The Demon soon to be revealed. He opened the box, and the counter-catalyst, this golden crystal, shone in the spotlight of the stage. Miles took it out quickly, and activated it with his power of The Aura, to the horror of this Demon. The golden bolt of energy exploded like a ball of sand on the Demon's chest, and she let forth an ungodly yell of terror and anger for her revealing. The crowd began to flee, in its expectedly panicked manner.

"Leave that camera!" Miles shouted at one of the men livestreaming the event. He thankfully obliged, and ran himself out as well. The Deceiver, unable to hold its form any longer, erupted in flame, to show the true form of the infiltrator of the Demon Hordes. Skin marbled in blood red and jet black, eyes of orange spite, and a blade as twisted as the mind that forged the lies it protected.

"You are a bold one, Aura Warrior." The Demon taunted. "You even look just like this mortal race."

"It always pained me, but you're wrong. I'm one of the idiots from this planet. And you have weaved your masters' will into this world enough."

The Demon seemed almost impressed. "A human to wield The Aura? You must be something else you don't even know about. It is no matter. The Dark Six will honor me, Avanchenvaldr, destroyer of Aura Warriors!"

Avanchenvaldr charged at Miles with its weapon, and the cutlass he was given on Orvitaire appeared in his hand to do battle. A battle of powers, as well as blades. Shields conjured, and released towards their foe. All the while, Miles ensured that camera kept running, kept showing the world just what they were dealing with, what they hadn't dealt with. Miles outfought

Avanchenvaldr soon enough, landing the right blows to the right places. A slice on the Demon's weapon hand, a side kick to its knee. A systematic deconstruction of this abomination's ability to fight on.

"Who are you to deny the Dark Six their prize?" Avanchenvaldr demanded. "I want to know just who's name will be among those that die the most painfully!"

"You and your ilk may call me Radien," Miles spat, and sliced Avanchenvaldr's throat wide open with his blade. Instead of blood, out poured fire like a geyser, straight up as the broken Demon's form collapsed in on itself, and became little more than a pile of ash. Ramming was heard at the door. SAS were making their way in, and Miles warped out before their breach. A pile of ash, and a streaming camera were all that stood in the ruined auditorium.

The world saw what happened. As soon as the fight broke out, breaking news all over took the video feed and broadcasted it to all the eyes and ears of the human race, and Miles soon knew exactly what happened to the Dark Six's servants after Avanchenvaldr's death. A broadcast of his own was now transmitted, an automatic recording, intercepting all channels, playing in all of Earth's languages.

"This message is for the human race of Earth, and will play across the planet upon the death of the Deceiver

Demon Avanchenvaldr. The animator you knew, who made what you thought was so innocent, was anything but. You may have been tipped off when someone you may know, a friend or family, suddenly seemed confused. As if they had no memory of why they stood where they were. Some celebrated, as their conversion was only recent, and now they are free. But others... people who served the Demons all their lives... they regained their minds from where they left off. Men and women alike, who's old bodies now had their young souls back. Souls that were stolen and substituted with that of a Demon of Hell. Make no mistake, this was the work of Demons. The answer of if we are alone is a resounding no. So far from no, so far indeed. A universe teeming with life, of good peoples, who fight this war against the Demons in shadow and sun. I've destroyed their link to Earth, that they would have used as a front for their invasion of all creation. But now it falls to you to become a part of this universe. Some former Demon's servants have lost only a few days. Others, entire years, or even a whole lifetime. They will be hurt. They will hurt from what they have done beyond their will. Whether you forgive them, or punish them, or whatever, the universe watches to see what the Human race is. I take my leave now, and the rest is yours. I do truly hope I will be proven right to have shown you all this."

The message was across the world, and Miles decided it was time for him to leave it. There was indeed a whole universe out there, teeming with life and good peoples. With The Aura, Miles had time to match his ambitions. The Fourteen Werewolves closed for business, the tools and Techbooth moved to a storage on Cynofrax, courtesy of The Aura Runner's pocket dimension for a cargo bay.

Upon that arrival on Cynofrax, Miles beheld now Alindros city-province, the capitol of the world. Sorrenikas was only the second largest on the planet. He froze where he stood on the sidewalk, only just having his next great realization.

"I've got stories now," Miles said to himself aloud. "I... I have things I can tell others. I can walk among the stars, and tell them what I see. I could have allies. I could have... so much that I don't even have words for. I ran out of tears so many years ago on the stories I'd never be able to relate to..."

A familiar-feeling Redarian stopped in his tracks as he saw Miles gaze out upon the cityscape. "Radien?"

"Jarrek," Miles responded, still his eyes spaced out, staring at everything. "I don't even have words for what I have now, because I so understood for so long that I never would... that changes now. I don't even know what this feeling is. I don't know if it's good or bad.

I... I just don't know."

Jarrek walked up to Miles, looking him in the eye as Miles re-focused himself, now to the Redarian before him. "My people have a word for what you're feeling: Raiyaan. The literal translation is 'finally'. But it means more than that, I'm sure you can figure."

"I suppose so," Miles said. "A state so much of 'at long last,' but I don't even know what I'm finally getting, because the very idea of it never existed to me. I don't... I don't..."

"Don't try to, then," Jarrek said, putting a hand on Miles's shoulder. "Don't try to know today. You don't need to know today. Not even tomorrow. You only need to know when you figure it out yourself."

"Figure it out myself... I've never really gotten to do that."

"Clearly you need some time. Just raw time. Come with me." Jarrek showed Miles just outside Alindros, a small cave. No telling if it was natural or not. "This is a Font. It's a well of cosmic power, without any real refinement or name, or anything. It's basically raw universe. They're pretty common. In fact, it's rare to find a planet without one. I was recently on a planet completely barren of a single Font, and take a wild guess which."

Miles looked over to the Redarian, knowing well it

was Earth.

"It's incredible you're still alive," Jarrek admired. "You've got an inherent connection, a higher understanding of what is and should be, and must never. The universe doesn't make more sense to you, you just know better than most that it doesn't have to. A mind like that, on a planet like Earth... it's a wonder you aren't completely insane by now as the rest of your species is just so slow, and rigid, and spiteful."

A moment passed, and Miles looked to the Font. A pool of deep blue, liquid power that seemed to bleed from the crust of Cynofrax itself, but it never overflowed from the natural cistern it formed.

"Radien, you're clearly more. Human could never describe you. Human denotes a creature of that spite, that sadistic love to crush what is genuinely pure and good. I could never call you among that. It took less than five minutes when I first saw you to know that. You've only proved it further."

Miles looked back at Jarrek. "I only don't know what to say, because I've never had to think of what to say in a... position like this. It seems... impossible to think someone could ever tell me that."

"I'll leave you to it, then," Jarrek said, with a smile and friendly slap on the shoulder. "Do what you know you understand, take the time you need, because you clearly do."

Miles touched where Jarrek hit gently, practically scoffing to himself, it seemed so ridiculous, such casual friendship. But the Font was before him. Miles approached the Font, and placed a single foot inside its... water? It sure felt like water. Once again, time stopped like it had on Earth that one time.

"It's not that I need a lot of *time*," he said aloud, to himself again. "It's that *I* need a lot of time. I can count to five, and it's still a five-count."

"Now you're getting it." The voice of The Aura made itself known. "A higher understanding indeed."

"But you're not literally The Aura," Miles postulated. "Perhaps the manifestation my mind has made is an interpretation of the power, your voice is different than the Prism. But the Prism only holds the key."

"Continue."

"But it doesn't need to be understood utterly and fully, the mystery doesn't need a yes or no to its question. What I understand is that whether you are the literal power of The Aura, or a voice my head created to help my consciousness interpret the universe around me, it does not change what you do. You still guide me. What does it matter if I call you The Aura, or I give you a name like a person? You guide me well, and that makes you The

Aura enough."

"There's not much I can say you don't already know, because Veralis and Jarrek already told you. Human fails to describe you, Radien. Once you leave this cave, time will return to its prior and normal pace. The rest is up to you."

Miles spent what would've been days if not for the Font's lock of time itself, meditating, pondering, determining. He then left, not far behind Jarrek.

"I'd say that was quick, but I know better," Jarrek commented. "Anything I should know?"

Miles didn't need to think this time, he already had plenty. "Not yet. But you'll be the second to know, given that I'll be the first."

Jarrek smirked with what must be a trademark witty smug of the Redarian people. "Quit wastin' time, then."

CHAPTER THE NINTH

Miles's next move was to return to Turazin and inform the Conclave of Sentience of Earth's situation. They were eager to hear his update, given that Demons were involved.

"The Deceiver Demon Avanchenvaldr is slain, and the Dark Six's hold on Earth is broken," Miles began, to the sighs of relief from the rest of the Conclave's members. "Those under their control have indeed regressed to their prior selves from before, and I have left Earth in its own hands, with no intent to return. Though, I would wish to be informed of any further matters that end up concerning the planet." Several present nodded understandingly.

"Avanchenvaldr? Was that the Demon's name?" a

Hykentiu asked, leaning over from almost the other end of the long table, admittedly poorly designed for Conclaves. Perhaps this was an old table, that no one bothered to replace as time went on. A selachimorph standing bipedal was a little odd, but his body clearly made it work.

"Aye," Miles confirmed. "It gave me that name itself before my duel with it."

The Hykentiu let out a sound that would probably be what one would do to give the message of a half-frustrated growl underwater, where traditional sound tends to not really work. "Avanchenvaldr plagued Pogo-Pira for centuries, and it now makes sense that *it* was on Earth. The methods are all just rehashes of what *it* did on the Hydenti and Hykentiu home world to wrest control. I would've liked to see that *Klee-an* die."

"Consider this your lucky day, then." Miles tossed a data drive containing the video from Edinburgh to the young warrior, which he eagerly caught, and pocketed.

"Anyways—" the Loriken from the last meeting interjected. "With Avanchenvaldr dead, that's the last of the known Demons on record. The Dark Six have lost their last connection we know of to reality. It will take them a good while before they can make another proper move."

"Correct, but we should not think this as their

grand defeat," a Laksorian assured. The yellow-furred lapin appeared to have some kind of scientific wear that Miles could draw the connection to. Sure, it wasn't a white lab coat of Earth, but it was clear this woman was a scientist. "The Dark Six batter at the walls of reality every moment, and while they seldom breach, a breach it remains. We can sure as hell relax, but let's not be complacent."

"I agree with..," Miles started.

"Jaden."

"I agree with Jaden, then. Whatever all your plans are, I'm going to participate in this universe I've just been shown."

As if Miles had said something profound, the entire Conclave fell silent, looking to him as if they couldn't believe he just said that.

"Have I offended?" Miles said, a little worried.

"Your surname, it's Radien, correct?" the Hykentiu asked. Miles nodded, and both paused. "Brothers and sisters of the Conclave... we all are familiar with the Old Cynofraxian word 'Rayd,' and the suffix '-ien'?"

"We should not press upon that now," Jaden interrupted. "We must not be so quick to... try to find the new one."

The Conclave quickly adjourned, and Miles caught

up with the Hykentiu at the building's pub, who admittedly had a lot more tone to his muscle than first noticed. "I never got your name, but what was Jaden on about?"

"I'm Miirkae," he informed, then taking a swig from a glass full of cloudy drink. "Jaden was on about Caltoran."

Miles asked for a glass of botanical distillate, hoping it would get him something near to gin. "Keep in mind, I only just got here when it comes to anything beyond planet-scale matters."

Miirkae continued as Miles sipped from what was probably gin. It was close enough. The bottle was labeled 'Kalisaine's Root'. "Caltoran was a hero to many, many worlds, even whole galaxies. Towns and provinces had their champions, planets have folk heroes, and the universe had Caltoran, its defender. He was killed rather recently, but he had honestly died a good while before then."

Miirkae downed whatever was in his glass, then another as he recounted what was clearly a painful story. "A Demon killed him like a coward. Shot him from far away, in the aftermath of a skirmish. Didn't even have the balls to finish him up close. Just kept shooting as he moved forward, making sure he was dead, because he was just that fuckin' scared of what Caltoran would do if he were alive to defend himself. The Dark Six took Caltoran's body after that. Used it, and his high status to take the universe by surprise. Hundreds of thousands of worlds burned a day by Caltoran's power, now under the control of the Dark fucking Six. Not even, I think. Just some Demon pawn, just like our Caltoran became. It took some of the most twisted and forbidden weapons the universe has ever devised just to bring him down, a second time, even..."

Miles took a drink from his own glass, and looked to Miirkae. "I know that saying I'm sorry is rather useless here. But if there were a different word I knew, I'd use that."

"I get it. And for it, thanks." This young warrior indeed, fit and prime, certainly seemed as though while he was appreciative to have his skill and his physique, likely regretted its necessity. "I hope you don't mind if I just call you Radien. I figure most people will be doing that, it's a little more palatable than Miles."

"Of course," Miles responded with a slight smile. "I suppose if I had the choice, Radien is more... legend-sounding." Miirkae laughed at that in agreement, and eventually went their own ways. Miles then headed to The Hideout, finally meeting Xenidar in person. Xenidar was only about up to Miles's ribs in height, and Miles wasn't any taller than five foot six. But Miles had been the shortest in the room many times before, so he had no plans to hold it against the Talvas Vulpian.

"Good to meet you in person, Radien," Xenidar greeted. "What can I help you with?"

"What can you tell me about that Laksorian from the Conclave, and her relation to Caltoran?"

Xenidar was almost surprised, but not quite. "It's not difficult to tell that they were good friends. What eats at her most is how much people insisted she be kept away from the corrupted body of a once honorable Laksorian. She was practically forced to inaction, as one of Laksor's leading minds behind Genome Hacking."

"That'd burn anyone, primordially," Miles quickly commented. "Lemme guess: Everyone said she was too valuable to risk losing, and made sure she wouldn't be, by any means?" To which Xenidar solemnly nodded. He sure didn't agree with the idea. "Well, I suppose that's what I needed to know for now."

An alarm blared, and Xenidar groaned. "Only two buildings on this whole damn planet, and still they can't be arsed to leave it alone!"

"Demons?" Miles asked.

"Thank the gods, no. Just a token group of anarchist-pirate... whatever the hell. The void between stars never seems to run out of jackasses after the information I guard here." Xenidar leaned over his desk and pressed a button, flipping several terminals over to reveal weapons, both melee and ranged of multiple styles and munitions. "Everyone who's willing, grab your favorite and get ready to defend The Hideout! Scanners show about a quarter-armada, mixed craft. Orbital defenses should keep all but... I'd say a couple thousand from hitting the ground."

To Miles's surprise, no one started to leave via the teleport bays in the building. Then again, Miles didn't exactly come from a planet known for producing loyal creatures. Time for him to be better. His Orvitarian Collapse Rifle conjured in his hands, courtesy of The Aura. Xenidar looked over and nodded in approval of the weapon, ready to open the door of The Hideout to its attackers, to which Miles was confused.

"That door wouldn't hold them for long, and it's not cheap to replace it. If it makes no difference, then we can at least spare ourselves that," Xenidar commented, clearly noticing Miles's confusion, followed by resolve as he raised his weapon.

The door opened, and the firefight began. Everyone inside The Hideout fired at the open door from their cover, shredding many of the attackers with bullets, lasers and bolts of plasma. Miles's rifle was in its close-range mode, and thus capable of full auto. He was able to pick off several of these lightly armored goons throwing themselves at the door, hardly even trying to use their compatriot's corpses as cover, which worried him, wondering if these men were just a diversion.

"Xenidar! Where are they trying to get to?" Miles shouted to the Talvas Vulpian, who was kneecapping targets with a corner-rifle of some kind.

"Well, they're just trying to get in to take over! If they got to the security hub, they'd pretty much secure this place! But this is the only way in, and they're using it!"

Miles gave Xenidar the kind of look an intelligent action hero gives the idiot who overlooked something obvious, and bolted off, following the signs for the security hub. "Techbooth, get me a map of this place, and all routes to the security hub!" He quickly ordered with the earpiece he wore, still connected to that machine that was just on Cynofrax now, at Veralis's home in Kaldres-Viane. The earpiece became a single-lens glass over his left eye, showing him the route to the security hub, and a readout:

ONE ESCAPE ROUTE ON PUBLIC PLANS EXISTS WITH A SMALL GUARD CONTINGENT, SLIGHTLY LONGER ROUTE FROM ENTRANCE TO SECURITY HUB.

Miles looked through the door to the hub, and saw the empty room, then started making his way towards the emergency exit, as it were. He rounded a corner and saw at least a dozen forms, far more heavily armored than the ones at the entrance, casually making their way to the security hub, having dealt with the fewer guards along the way. A burst of snap-fire later, and one was down, before Miles had to duck back to avoid the retaliation. Only one way to that hub now, and that was through him.

He made the motion to conjure The Aura's energy, but what would've been a flame fizzled instead. The readout from Techbooth: THE HIDEOUT'S INNER HALLS ARE SURROUNDED BY A VOID EMULATOR, RENDERING ACTIVE COSMIC POWER USELESS.

"I think I just figured that out, thanks," Miles quickly said to himself. He looked to his belt, as if expecting some grenades to conveniently appear like he actually had literal foresight to know this battle was coming. No dice, though.

"Ugh, fine," Miles grumbled, and the suppressive fire stopped from the other side of the corner. Footsteps. The first real combat. Avanchenvaldr was a duel the Demon already thought they won. The others were thugs or idiots. Time to see what he was made of.

The tip of a laser rifle peeked out next to Miles, and he went for it, driving the tip away from him with the palm of his hand, and drawing the AZP-621 pistol on his hip, blasting the man in front of him, then kicking the lifeless form back into his friends, while shooting the one immediately next to him. Two more shots, and the two that weren't in front of the careening corpse were down. A shot to one of them on the ground, leaving the other to struggle with the weight of a whole body as Miles charged forward. A shoulder roll to drop himself down as his opponents finally reacted to his presence and fired, and Miles came up right in front of his next two quarries, shooting one immediately, and grabbing the other, putting this armored shield of a body in front of the shots his friends in the back just let loose. Six shots and four fresh bodies later, and Miles let go of his cover and began to walk back towards the entrance, executing the one trapped under bodies from before.

The whole fight lasted less than fifteen seconds.

Miles was almost back to the main entrance when Xenidar showed up. "The rest have retreated. Whatever you did, it made them know they lost."

Miles looked at the hall full of heavily armored bodies. Heavily armored, but still very much dead. Xenidar seemed confused, not at their existence, but rather that they got as far as they did. "How the hell would the Rowdy Armada get armor like that, let alone men trained to use it? Thanks for the assist by the way Radien, and I'll deal with the rest, including the investigation into these guys."

Miles nodded, and headed out, warping back to Cynofrax, and his new base in Kaldres-Viane. There he stood, contemplating. Not about the people he killed that day, gods no. It wasn't a new idea to him, even before The Aura. Once again he contemplated this whole new universe before him. Perhaps that was what he was going to be doing between things to do. No, he rejected that. Contemplation was for later, and he'd done plenty already. He warped himself to Orvitaire, the planet Veralis said he'd enjoy on a proper visit. The Taigron armsmaster was coincidentally the first person he saw.

"Radien, is it?" she asked. Miles nodded. "Veralis thought a person like you might be back soon enough."

"Aye, and I wonder why she thought that?"

She introduced herself as Lyrais Kenteros, then explained herself. "Veralis, among other words, described you as 'Gival-Rokirien'. It's a Vulpian word, roughly meaning 'fighter with no fight to be fought'. Orvitaire is not called the Martial Planet for nothing. Peoples from across the universe come here to hone their skills as warriors, and as good men and women, and all in between or around. Just about every town has an arena, ours is over there." Lyrais pointed to a nearby building, more akin to a townhouse than a colosseum, but if the whole planet was fighters, then that made sense.

Miles thanked Lyrais for the information, and made his way to this arena. Sure enough, it almost was more like a townhouse, even with its own restaurant, but also multiple rings set up for sparring. Some people were on the side, shouting advice and betting drink purchases as they waited their own turn. Miles stood patiently on those sidelines, and a few others, likely regulars, noticed the odd man out.

"Hey, you want a match?" one asked, to Miles's surprise.

"Well, I'm not exactly here to write a treatise am I?" To which a good portion of the crowd cheered, once again surprising Miles that this was his welcome, rather than a boot out the door. One of the crowd suddenly shouted 'Run the gauntlet!,' and soon enough, the whole arena was roaring that phrase. 'Run the gauntlet! Run the gauntlet!"

"I sure can't go refusing that, then!" Miles excitedly proclaimed, to everyone's approval. The Gauntlet, it turned out, was fifteen fighters, one at a time. Either last for three minutes, or make them yield, whichever came first. The first match was honestly the hardest, as the adrenaline-induced twitchyness was causing some of his actions to be a little more exaggerated than he'd have liked. On one occasion during that match, he moved his leg a little too far and fast to check a kick, and almost lost his balance entirely. That one went to time. By the third, he was in his rhythm, forcing this and the next few opponents to yield. But even with The Aura, he could tire, even though it'd take a while.

Eventually came his last opponent, the fifteenth of The Gauntlet. The two eventually took each other to the ground, not Miles's favored position, but he was making it hell to keep him there, escaping a hold here, pinning a limb to his chest there, just making sure the Loriken atop him couldn't get that final lock, and the bell finally rang, to the cheers of the crowd, and Miles flopping back, utterly winded. So was his opponent, too, it seemed. The Loriken flopped on top of him.

"Buy me a drink first," Miles said, and the two laughed as they pulled themselves up.

"Is that an offer?" she asked, soon after introducing herself as Nirial. Miles was once again surprised, and rather stammered out his response, with a message adding up to 'Possibly?' Nirial must've seen something in that confusing set of jabbered words, because she then suddenly caught Miles in her arms with a hug, and he nearly jumped out of his skin in shock. After that was dealt with, Miles cleared his throat.

"Thanks," he said. "I think I owe you now." Nirial shook her head and assured that all was well. It honestly was unlikely that the universe was odd, more that Miles had just grown up on a particularly shitty planet. The worst kind of lethal, that doesn't even have the gall to stab you in the front, but instead has to hide behind a scope a mile away because they're that afraid of a fair fight. Unfortunately, it's also well understood that the moral high ground doesn't do the dead any favors.

Orvitaire was certainly a haven world in many ways. Miles even learned a bit about its history, and that the first colonists on the planet were warriors and philosophers who had fled their home world to safely practice their crafts and hone their skills, after the sheer bureaucracy and near-totalitarianism back home made it impossible to lift a finger in your own defense without repercussions as if you started the fight, regardless of anything.

They came to Orvitaire to just be decent. Of course, this was many millions of years ago, before self-defense was recognized as an essential right across the stars. And the stars were clearly better for that right of one's own protection. Miles couldn't help but feel like he was coming into the game rather late, when all the questions had an answer now, with a huge and sensitive history of conflict for them all. In a universe as big as this, there had likely been a war over everything by now. But at least these people were understanding, and didn't expect perfection and infallibility in all actions at all times.

Veralis wasn't slow to pull Radien out of this ridiculous contemplation. "You've got a universe to participate in, not ponder about," she said, having successfully snuck up on him somehow.

"And I suppose you have something to tell me in that regard?" Miles said, finishing the drink he had gotten to having. Veralis placed a small video player in front of him. Miles activated it, and Jaden showed on the screen.

"I'm wondering if you can help me find a few components for a project of mine I'm working on, codename 'Gama,' the anachronism for the device I'm trying to build," Jaden greeted. Miles looked over to Veralis, who assured him that she could be trusted.

"I'm listening," Miles replied.

"The GAMA device, or Genome Assimilation-Manipulation Apparatus, banks itself on the principle of DNA strands simply being lines of code associated with chemicals, that in theory, can be changed by removing chemicals and replacing them with new ones. For example, if the chemical string ABCDE leads to yellow fur coloring, one might swap chemical A with chemical F and get, say, green fur."

"I understand the principle, but what do you need me for?"

"My prototype is able to map the genome in less than a second. However, the actual operation of hacking the genome currently looks to take years on a single voluntary subject. What I need is a tech that can make that process quicker, and I've narrowed down some candidates."

Three devices showed themselves onscreen, labeled "TAIGRON E-GEAR OPTIMIZER", "REDARIAN BIO-INTEGRATOR", and "HAJIVAKK BLOODSTREAM ACCELERANT MODULE". The third of these had a red border to signify that it was likely to be the most helpful, and most difficult to attain.

"I just need those items, and I can figure out everything else. You'll be rewarded well for each, and even more so if you manage to get them all."

Miles was a little confused about the reward aspect of things, and turned to Veralis, who, outside of frame, made a circle with one hand and pointed her index finger through it, which now added surprise to Miles's confusion. He turned back to Jaden.

"I'll see what I can do. Should I expect resistance, or is there a different reason you're not doing this yourself?"

"I'm up to my eyes with other work, and getting other parts on my own. This will just streamline the process, and wouldn't go unappreciated."

Miles nodded. "I'll see what I can do." To which Jaden thanked, and the video comm switched off. Miles turned to Veralis. "Really? Like... actually?"

Veralis shrugged. "Laksorians are like that sometimes. Most species in the universe rather understand the pointlessness of most traditional currency systems, so trades are often made in things needed now, favors for later, or services immediately. For her, she honestly might think she's offering lower than average."

"Right. Can I expect your input or help on this?"

"She asked you, so that's up to you," Veralis replied, and Miles nodded in a 'fair enough' manner before beginning his planning. The first two could be acquired through common trade, from the looks of it, but the Hajivakk Bloodstream Accelerant Module... that was an experimental medical device, and likely wouldn't be available to him just asking as a random dude, so Miles asked Veralis to get the common items, while he handled the challenging task, a test for himself. She agreed, and Miles took himself to Caren'Das, the capital world of the leopard-like Hajivakk people, or Haji-Son, depending on the context. Hajivakk was just the name of the species, and Haji-Son were who they are as people. The sum of their morals, ideals, and accomplishments.

On arrival, Miles did some research to find who

had access to the Accelerant Modules. He wasn't planning to actually take one as much as figure out exactly how to make a new one. He was basically going to pirate the machine, like one pirates software. He needed to get close enough to hit it with a Lidar (or Light-Radar) Scan-Pulse, and get a full 3D model and composition map of the module, to deconstruct it electronically, and make one of his own.

After finding out the actual manufacturer of these devices, he made up a disguise as one of their maintenance technicians, and went into the research lab, posing as one for a surprise inspection, on the suspicion that some of the machines may have been using outdated software. Surprisingly, that worked, and he was left alone with the machine. It was actually more like a chip than a device, but a chip attached to an intravenous introduction device, to speed up the actual process of the bloodstream. The idea, it seemed, was to make the actual bodily processes work faster for a short time, essentially prematurely aging and destroying bacterial infections without adversely affecting the patient, as long as enough quantity of a fresh blood transfer could be assured.

Miles's Lidar Scanner was able to completely map the device, and its elemental composition and electronic programming, then sending the schematic to his

Keystone Forge. He assured the Hajivakk doctors that all was well on the check, and he was relieved to find out the alarm was false, at least on that one. A trip back to Cynofrax, and the Keystone Forge in Kaldres-Viane later, and he now had a perfect bootleg Hajivakk Bloodstream Accelerant Module, soon bringing it to Jaden's lab on Redaria Omega, the neighboring planet to Laksor itself.

"Maybe I would download a car," Miles said to himself before Jaden noticed his return.

"That was... alarmingly quick. How did you get ahold of it so without incident?" Jaden asked, impressed.

"Applied cleverness and a Lidar Scan-Pulse," Miles answered. "Now, that thing is the tech you're looking for in all but manufacturer. It turns out these things are being made by a single company, and that right there is essentially a perfect bootleg."

"Perfect bootleg? That sounds like an oxymoron," Jaden said, almost worried as she plugged the module into an almost downright sinister-looking device, like a space-age Iron Maiden. The worry was quickly quelled, however, when what was likely the GAMA machine powered up without a hitch.

"Yeah, but I did once hustle DVDs in middle school. My setup allowed me to perfectly rip the discs and burn them onto new ones with no change in quality to either. It helped that my father had a weekly free rental from his work."

Jaden looked very confused.

"I just realized that DVDs are an Earth-unique term," Miles said aloud. "But anyways, I'd still be cautious about that. Apparently even the 'legit' ones are still experimental."

The GAMA device powered up, and ran a system check. All things were in order. "Actually, it's more just a controversial tech. People have tried to make... well, this idea before. To speed up the process of the bloodstream and its natural detoxification system, but it's often resulted in next level strokes and heart attacks. This thing works, it's just difficult to convince the public after the times that it didn't, despite similar assurance," Jaden explained as she configured the machine. "By the way, I do need a volunteer for an inaugural run of this device. You never have liked being human, did you?"

"Not a day in my life I felt anything but disgraced to be human," Miles affirmed.

"So becoming Laksorian would be an improvement, then?" Jaden quickly asked.

"Undoubtedly. But there's clearly lots of species in the universe, and I'll need time to think about which one to—"

"I think I can eliminate that time for you. There are no cons to going Laksorian, only ever benefits."

Jaden was clearly excited about the idea of turning Miles into one of her kinsmen, almost unnervingly so.

"I understand, Jaden. Just... give me some time enough to make that call myself, all right?" Miles implored, to which Jaden agreed, as if pulling herself back from a different state of being. "Make no mistake, Jaden. You've honored me with this offer. I won't forget it, and when I've made my choice, I hope you won't have, either."

They said their goodbyes, or more like 'till next time's, and Miles warped over to Redaria Prime, the neighboring planet in this solar system called the Velani Array. Apparently, it was a happening place. Miles was able to quickly verify those claims, and have himself some well-earned R&R.

CHAPTER THE TENTH

The Aura had clearly given Miles a boost to his ability to metabolize, because the drinks weren't having much an effect on him. That wasn't a bad thing, of course. In fact, a hell of a blessing to never really be able to get beyond just lightly buzzed. Someone sat next to him, which seemed odd, until he took a quick look and saw the Hykentiu Miirkae.

"I took a look at the footage of you taking down Avanchenvaldr," he started. "I think the term for how it's doing on Pogo-Pira is... viral. It's given a lot of closure for a lot of people, and that sendoff wasn't half-bad, either."

"I can't imagine you've come from Turazin just to tell me that," Miles replied, appreciating that he was able to do something helpful for Miirkae's people.

"Not entirely, but that was the main point I wanted to make." Miles had a little trouble swallowing that, and the Redarian Ale he had a mouthful of.

"I'm... not entirely sure what you meant by that."

"Well, I figured I could also let you know that there's a group of Hykentiu Demon Hunters on Gliropa that while their record is impressive, there's been some doubts about their continued loyalty, and most of the leadership of both planets are too worried about their continued positions of power to actually do anything about it. They don't want to end up being wrong, so they won't risk it," Miirkae explained, while showing Miles a screen with bios of each member of this group, known as the Chorgon Nehr.

"This seems like the kind of thing you might've told me about first," Miles noted with another sip of drink.

"Not really. It was way more important for you to know how much you've done for the Hykentiu people." Miirkae then turned towards the bar for an order. "Cloudburster, please."

Another surprise for Miles on the ways the universe preferred to work. "I'd argue, but I doubt there's a point to it. I guess I've lived too long figuring the next task was more important than how one did on the prior." Miirkae nodded to this affirmingly, and Miles scrolled through the Demon Hunter's dossiers. "But why are people doubting the Chorgon Nehr? Like you said, their record is clearly impressive."

"That's the thing. The Chorgon Nehr isn't the problem, their doubters are. Loud minorities on the Galus-Net seem to be intent on a slander mission, choosing to highlight their minor missteps in the past over noticing their actions in the present. And unfortunately, they're gaining supporters. Gliropa's authorities and leaders have no plans to denounce the Chorgon Nehr, but they can't seem to grow a set and call out these idiots who clearly haven't even been on the same planet as a Demonic incursion."

Miles scrolled through, noticing in particular a single incident where the Chorgon Nehr destroyed an entire attacking force of Demons, but friendly fire wounded accidentally a couple of bystanders, with at most a single fatality. Some called for the dissolving of the defense force, not even paying attention to that the next of kin to the victims were compensated far beyond reasonable doubt with funerary arrangements and monetary payout. "Damn, even the families of accidental friendly-fire victims are calling foul on the dissenters. You sure can't honor the dead by turning them into weapons for the living."

"And that's almost word-for-word what the

families are saying," Miirkae added, taking back the screen once Miles handed it over, then taking a drink. "These bastards can't be dealt with traditionally, or they'll say shit like it's proving their point. Someone on the outside needs to find some way to get them to quit whining over resolved issues that they didn't even have a part in."

"Just don't let these guys see Earth, they'll get ideas. I've unfortunately had to see my share of fools like that. I never did figure out anything solid beyond quiet assassination. Not that I acted on it, this was before I had The Aura. I'll certainly do what I can to make sure no one has to die, because I might have some proper ideas how to shut them up beyond tearing out vocal chords."

Miirkae took a decent drink of his Cloudburster, clearly his favored cocktail since that's what he was drinking back on Turazin before remarking "Radien, you've got some very creative ways of ending people, are you sure you're not from Raon-Arashal or Zharekk?"

"I wish" was the response.

"But then again, I might not know as well as I do a fool when I see or hear of one," Miles continued. "I'll finish my stuff here, then head to Gliropa."

"There is no rush here," Miirkae said. "That's why it was the second thing I told you about. And that's also why I'm gonna stay here if that's fine by you."

"Of course. And perhaps we can talk of things other than fools and Demons." The two laughed and had their drinks, food, and conversation. Miles even played a set on this hangout's stage when he learned they were having their equivalent of an open mic, and had one of those Replicators like in Kaldres-Viane. After that, he and Miirkae went their separate ways, Miles warping back to Veralis's home, and heading to the Holographic Arena he relocated from Earth for some training. Miles tended to get lost in this for a while, as he genuinely enjoyed honing his skill like this, and Veralis had to switch the arena off to get his attention when she entered the room.

"I had him!" Miles exclaimed when his opponent disintegrated prematurely.

"That's why I was willing to turn this off now," Veralis remarked, leaning on the projector with a rather oddly high amount of smug. "I want a turn, move your butt outta here."

"Make me."

It was as if that was the response she was hoping for, and the impromptu spar began as Veralis walked over calmly, before leaping forward with the kind of push kick that starts most fights in high-octane action movies. Miles dodged out of the way, and threw his leg out to sweep Veralis's that she was standing on, but missed since she was that much taller than him. The miscalculation gave her the time to reposition and retaliate, but the fist was swept away with the back of Miles's hand. The two began their dance from there, as if fencing with single hands to see who had more control, who had more precision to their credit, before the tactic was broken by an attempted tackle from the Vulpian, and Miles's subsequent sprawl. He managed to wrap his arms around and lift her entirely off the ground, only to drop the both of them back down, and roll backwards into the full mount. Veralis quickly reversed the positions by pinning their bodies together and throwing her hips over to roll on top of Miles, and Miles simply made sure no progress could be made by pinning her arms, or parrying them out of the way, making it nearly not worth it to keep him on the ground. Veralis dove off, and both stood up, striking threatening and stylistic poses at each other, before both burst out laughing.

"All right, have fun," Miles eventually said, and left her to it.

"You've gotten way better," Veralis commented as she configured her settings for the Arena.

"I still don't like ground fighting."

"Then I can see why you like to make it so much hell to keep you there. Make it not worth the time, so everyone's better of just doing it the old-fashioned way."

Miles nodded, and decided to lay on his bed for a bit, even though he didn't actually *need* to sleep, he could if he wanted to. But he was just planning to lay there for a bit, until he had a better idea. Eventually, he decided to head to Gliropa and deal with the Chorgon Nehr's dissenters.

First was a meeting with the contact Miirkae noted, by the name of Dorg.

"The problem with these buggers, as I'm sure Miirkae already established, is that they're in a position with nothing to lose and everything to gain. If any of Gliropa or Pogo-Pira's authorities do anything about these dissenters, it'll give them all kinds of ammo to spew," Dorg established, while a list of the known dissenters of the Chorgon Nehr scrolled by on a screen.

"Miirkae told me of this. The method I figured barely has a chance of working, because the problem is that the crazier they are, the more potently they'll use any excuse they have. I've seen this special kind of manipulative before, on Earth. They'll never be the ones to throw a punch first, but will utterly goad you into being the one who only technically started fighting," Miles said those last words with a tone of massive disdain, to show just how unbelievably infuriating he found such people. "We need to find a central point for them, ideally location. Like, is there a city that contains only these cosmic cancelers? A hideout or building or semi-secret lair they rub their hands plottingly in?"

Dorg thought for a moment, then brought up a new window on the screen. "Sort of. There's an event in Hulae upcoming that, while it says its an expo for 'new social ideas' and what have you, it's just a big meet-up for them to all agree with each other that anything other than perfection is evil forever, unless they themselves do it."

Miles started to think.

"We already thought about something like that, but even with the majority who'd be happy to see those dimwits gone, it's too risky for collateral," Dorg cut in.

"No, I wasn't thinking to bomb them. I have a different idea. So, it looks like these people practically take over the entire downtown?"

"Just about," Dorg explained, curious to see what Miles was coming up with. "They have a frankly strange amount of funds, so they rent several blocks worth of buildings. Thing is, we know we need to act soon, because everyone else is getting restless about these ridiculous dissenters. And they're not just on about the Chorgon Nehr. This expo is almost a solar system's worth of people who's hardest decisions in life was which well-respected person to attack next over a discretion from half a lifetime ago. I don't know why they do it. Jealousy?

Ease of effectiveness?"

"Dorg, what's the problem you were going to tell me about?" Miles said to set the Hykentiu back on track.

"Right. There's a lot of backlash against these guys from the everymen of this sector. Business owners in the Hulae board up their shops and take vacations for the duration of this expo so that they don't have to hear a word from their insufferable mouths. But words have been that people are gearing up to fight them proper. 'Show them real problems' as it were. We don't want this civil war on our hands, there's plenty of things to worry about as it is."

"But there's a non-zero amount of time where a large area has *nothing* but these people?"

Dorg nodded, and Miles explained himself.

"If we isolate the area that fits that criteria, basically nothing but Chorgon Nehr dissenters and other Space SJWs, I think we should try to force some kind of crisis on them. One that they can't run away from by leaving their expo, one they have to endure. But it'd need to look natural. There can't be any room for postulating that we're behind it."

Dorg was very confused at the Earth slang Miles used to describe this group that would have downtown Hulae, but seemed to get the idea.

"Either they burn in the crisis, or grow a damn set.

No matter which, the amount of people being this shitty decreases massively. I've been doing this on a much smaller scale on Earth for a while. Making absolute fools of the kind of people who would insist on 'civil discussion' with slave owners, because they underneath it totally want to own slaves, but know they'd get decked if they admitted it. I can only imagine how many flavors of those kinds of people there's gonna be in Hulae."

Dorg nodded solemnly. "I don't even want to guess. I'll trust you to figure it out then, and don't tell me what specifically you're gonna do. Ideally, I don't even want to be able to guess what your involvement was. Makes less loose ends," Miles agreed and headed out, renting a room in the industrial sector of Hulae. Cheaper, and surprisingly decent.

During the night, he almost flustered himself trying to think up his plan, until he finally had one, but it was admittedly the last one he wanted to use. But by the time he needed to be making moves, it was all he had. He sighed before he left for downtown with a briefcase-concealed device that honestly, he'd rather not have resorted to.

He arrived via private bus, commissioned by one of the groups present at this event called "Torgaen's Unfound", or something. His plan was to head into the center of the downtown square, and activate a containment grid around the place, cutting them off from the rest of the planet. The make of the device was obscure enough that no species or planet could be pinned with what was about to happen, this siege from within.

Something felt off, though. A new player, not previously known had entered the game, so to speak. Miles's eyes darted around, trying to figure out what The Aura seemed intent to warn him about.

In the distance, a lone Loriken was setting up something of his own. Not a bomb, that was for sure, but it was definitely not the power generator its label plate was trying to say. He made his way over.

"I'm just setting up a power generator for some of the booths here, compliments of 'Ebsil Ty'." Time seemed to freeze, and the letters he spoke, but may not have pronounced, appeared before Miles in the air, as if he was processing them just that quickly. EBSL TJY. A single shift in letter, DARK SIX.

It seemed Miles didn't need to create a crisis, this Demon servant was going to do it for him. Before Miles could act, the power turned on. "No, wait!" was too late of a call before a red portal tore itself into existence, forcing a gaping wound in the fabric of reality itself, and the Loriken was ripped to shreds, so close to this event. Miles dropped the briefcase he held, and conjured his cutlass as the first troopers from Hell stepped into existence. He began to face them, and cut them down, but he was only one man, and the Demons that ignored him began their slaughter as the crowd of this expo ran in terror, as they would.

Miles blasted his containment field generator with The Aura, and it activated, surrounding the downtown of Hulae, and there was no way out for anyone once it finished projecting itself. Miles's curses for this twisted luck of his, both fortunate and not at the same time were only interrupted by him slicing through another Demon. For some reason, there was no one else fighting but him. No other power-wielders, or even someone with a larger than average pocketknife. This initial bloodbath lasted for near ten minutes, as Demons streamed from the portal, and Miles tried to close it with The Aura somehow, hoping he could get lucky with the shots he fired at it. In a desperate moment, he pulled his hand back, as if trying to dislodge this accursed gate with telekinesis. It seemed to stutter in space at this, and Miles figured he was on to something. Another invisible heave, and the portal began to violently destabilize, crushing in on itself until nothing remained but the mangled corpse of the hellspawn that was trying to get through it at the moment. Fighting for a few moments more, he made his retreat, but the problem remained:

thousands of Demons were here, and there was no way Miles could let that containment grid down until that number was zero.

CHAPTER THE ELEVENTH

Miles's comm-link in his scanner pinged. It was Dorg. "Radien, *please* tell me this wasn't your plan! The Conclave is in an uproar, and everyone wants answers, especially me!"

"My plan was just the containment field! I was going for to lock 'em all in like a reverse siege or something, then some jackass Loriken opens this portal! And it wasn't pretty, either! It's like it... shredded itself into reality! There wasn't much left of the poor bastard by the time Demons actually started coming through..."

Dorg sighed in relief, that he hadn't made a huge mistake in believing anything of Miles. "What do I tell the Conclave, then? This is my corner of the galaxy to speak for, after all."

"My investigation into the Chorgon Nehr's dissenters led me to this event, and I took the containment grid generator in case things got hairy, because I figured that there'd be a considerable amount of people who'd want this lot dead, and at the very least it could be held in one spot until blowing over."

Dorg looked over his shoulder, nodded quickly, and cut off the transmission. By this point, it was several hours in, and Demons were patrolling the streets, looking for survivors. There weren't many, and they were holed up and hiding in the buildings that hadn't been searched yet. If nothing else, they probably wouldn't be speaking against Demon hunters anymore...

Miles nearly jumped out of his skin when someone put their hand on his shoulder, and almost got a knife to the throat. A Hajivakk, a more winter-acclimatized one to be sure. "Jesus fucking shit, man, don't startle me when Demons are out and about! I could've killed you!"

"Yeah, not my best move, I see that now," she noted. "I've not seen your kind before, what's your name?"

"What, now? This isn't exactly the best time, considering the factors!"

"Well, if we're gonna die here, I think I'd like to know a bit about this new species I'm seeing!"

Both fell silent as they heard footsteps. Their ears weren't the only ones listening, it seemed. The sound of metal shifting, like someone had propped their weapon on their shoulder, and the heavy breathing of a Demonic trooper were all that could be heard soon enough. Miles waited for a few moments, listening for where it was, before standing up and throwing the knife that would've gone into this clumsy native of the planet Mjarfus's throat into the abomination instead, and it decayed to rot and ash before it could hit the ground.

"I'd like to think I have no plans to die today," Miles said, turning back dramatically. "If you'd like to think that as well, stay close." Miles took two steps forward, then looked back around, as if to correct himself. "Wait, no, fuck off, you're one of the idiots attending this event! One of the asshats who'd rather the worlds did nothing while this kind of thing went down!"

"I beg to differ," she said, reaching into her dark grey sweater and producing a small badge, bearing an official-looking seal that Miles was probably supposed to recognize and think had meaning. "Synval-Kolderan, I'm here on behalf of the Chorgon Nehr, we've been tracking a Loriken with a Rift Lance for months, and our last lead was here, of all the rotten luck. Did you see where he went after the portal was opened?"

"Yeah, he went all over the place." Synval took a

second, then winced a little. "Probably figured Hulae's expo was the prime location, with a city full of people who unironically thought that Demons could be reasoned with, and had equitable desires, not even demands."

"Well, it was either me or someone who wasn't planning to leave without knocking a few heads." A shadowy figure seemed to creep across the wall behind them, like a deep-sea crab of ninety percent legs that didn't seem to work in any comforting way. Synval whipped around to face it, drawing a concealed pistol and blasting this Demon with a pulsing energy that caused it to writhe on the ground and disintegrate. "I think we can get along. You clearly don't agree with this lot either, and can handle yourself. That's all I need in an ally right now."

Miles nodded, and Synval took hold of her own scanner, that seemed tailor-made for Demon hunting, since it had an exact count of how many were left. Nine hundred eighty-seven, thanks to their separate efforts over the last few hours, and maybe a handful of desperate last stands from the less fortunate. Astonishingly, the Demons outnumbered the survivors. There were well over fifty thousand attending this event. But both of them understood that now was not the time to be burdened by death. The Demons sure wouldn't be, and had no problems taking advantage of anyone who was.

A finite number of foes, thus every blow dealt was permanent. Miles and Synval switched between operating together and independently, picking off lone foot soldiers, and teaming up for the occasional squad or particularly large opponent. The number of lifeforms in the downtown that weren't Demons however, reached only two. The first night rolled around, and unfortunately, it looked like they'd be stuck for a bit. Only fifty or so thinned from the horde. The opportunities were not plentiful, and as they made their threat to the attack's success known, the Demons were become more vigilant, and it was unlikely they were traveling alone from here on in. Miles and Synval had found a warehouse near the edge of the quarantine that the Demons weren't paying attention to, even if only because they'd already raided it hours before, and killed everyone inside. The only fortunate thing was that the bodies weren't even there to be seen all mangled, since the forces of Hell used bio-fuel to operate their war machines and artillery. Meaning of course, that cremation of the dead was going to be taken care of pretty thoroughly.

"Some cultures call it a high honor to have one's body burn after death," Synval said at their pseudo-campfire. It was more just a soft lantern. "The idea that they are useful even beyond mortal existence, as light or as fuel."

"And others?" Miles asked.

"Others say that to be reduced from a grand and complex form to simple ash is an insult. The universe is a big place, so there's all other views in between. I can't say for sure what this crowd's collective thought on it was. But I think most will be glad that they don't have to speculate why the casket had to be closed, as it were."

Miles nodded. "It's really odd that I'm so flung into this whole universe thing. It was less than a year ago I was so stuck on a backwater planet, so sure my whole life would be nothing but stagnant and unsatisfying. In these short months, I've been shown and granted so much, more than I think I could comprehend if I thought about it long enough."

"Probably shouldn't spend too much time thinking on it, then," Synval suggested. "It only matters where it came from sometimes. If you know well that your gifts came not from deliberate, needless pain, misfortune or fuckin' whatever, then you can just have your time and use it too, as far as I'm concerned."

"It seems to be the consensus around here. Far from what I've usually heard. All that 'life's to be suffered' bullshit from just about every religious jabroni to spit on the ground with their shoes, the idea that nothing is supposed to be good…" He chuckled for a second. "There was a disturbing amount of people who'd look at like, a kid's show that was actually solid, right? Y'know, funny stuff. Good memories. They'd then make these ridiculous theories that it's actually all death and misery. Like, 'the main character is hallucinating their friends' or 'everyone's dead and it's actually purgatory,' and the like"

Synval laughed, appalled. "Seriously?! That sounds so… ugh, I haven't even got a word for it! It's the kind of stupid shit you could only look at and laugh at the lame effort to ruin everyone's fun!"

Miles agreed, she hit the nail on the head with that. They then began to plan their efforts for the coming day, and the days ahead. And as the days went forward, the Demons were killed quicker and quicker as Miles learned more about them, the different variants, and how to dispatch them. Though initially, it was predicted it would take near a month to eliminate them all, the final Demon was dead within a week. The fact that they were still trying to have eyes everywhere with fewer numbers helped, as it spread them out quite thin. Synval showed Miles the count on her scanner. Zero Demonic presences remaining, and Miles nodded and let down the containment field. Synval said she would handle the press, and Miles left her to it, heading back to Cynofrax, flopping on the couch in Veralis's home, which she almost considered to be both of theirs, but Miles wasn't convinced, since he wasn't paying rent. Freeloader, maybe. He'd call himself that rather quickly.

Veralis walked in from the Holographic Arena, which could be used for more than just combat training, it could even make complex projections of scenarios to react to, or environments to navigate. She mussed Miles's hair a little, and to his own surprise, he didn't mind that much, just playfully batting at her arms with a 'njehhh' sound.

"I'd ask how it went, but I already know most of it," Veralis said, and Miles sighed.

"Yeah, could've been smoother. Kinda ironic that one of the Chorgon Nehr was actually helping me rid the Demons. It's probably going to help their cause a hell of a lot. A single Demon Hunter and some random yahoo took out a good twenty-five hundred Demons or so, and even closed the rift they were using."

Veralis switched Techbooth on to see the broadcast from Gliropa. Synval was making her address still, but Miles hadn't left her too long ago.

"I can confirm that a Rift Lance was used to open this portal, as the Chorgon Nehr had been tracking down leads on a possible attempt to construct it, and plans to use it to take over the entire planet of Gliropa. I am confident that if not for my intervention, and that of Miles Radien, whose presence was an honest miracle, the Demons would have at the very least destroyed Hulae in its entirety," she said to reporters, who themselves had to help hold back the crowd trying to sneak a peek at what was left of the downtown block.

"And what of the fifty thousand plus people that were attending this expo? Miles Radien's species only recently was even noted as existent by the Conclave, and how can they be trusted when he himself denounces them? How many—"

"One at a time, and you'll be lucky that I have answers for both of those so far. It is with sorrow I must report that Miles and I were the only survivors, and it is known that Demons do not leave behind the bodies they destroy. Almost three thousand Demons were present, and of all the people here, the only ones who fought were myself and him. If his actions today, and his destruction of the Deceiver Avanchenvaldr do not tell you his trustworthiness to aid the universe, then I must call you... fuckin' dumb as shit."

Miles cracked up at that final comment. "Oh, I like her. Ho boy, she should do interviews on Earth. It'd be a laugh riot, followed by idiots getting punched, probably."

Veralis snickered and Miles more or less came to his senses. "Well over fifty thousand dead is not a laughing matter, I know. But she gets the point across, what needs be known."

"I know what you mean," Veralis said, hopping over the back of the couch to sit next to him. "I'll be honest, no one with a rational inkling will get too choked up over these kinds of people dying. They won't celebrate, no one will. They won't brush off fifty thousand as a statistic, people are better than that. But what they will do, is understand that this is why orders like the Chorgon Nehr, or the Vindarr Valokoria, or the Ordus Gente exist: If they don't, this is what happens, and without the luxury of a decent ending."

Miles sort of... understood what she meant by people. It's why that was the word he heard. People referred to the ones of the universe, the configurations of being that are worth fighting for and alongside, maybe even in the name of. But there didn't have to be a matter of 'in the name of' anything, this is just what needed to be. A warrior, when a fight needs be fought. A defender, when a world needs defending. A healer, when an innocent needs healing, and a wiseman when a lesson need be taught.

Never cowardly or weak, *aldka Sehlkavhika, þsehlkoska*

<GREGOR FJELLREV>

Never ignorant or the liar, *aldka Sehlhaldn, þlurein*

Never corrupted, never evil, *aldka Sehlflown, aldka Sehlakarka*

For hope is brought on the wings of the Defender, *Gidaan taydeltn aravinda Giraydien*

Miles remembered those words from back on Earth he didn't have words to define. He remembered that one riff of his, Song of the Defender, that he had played on his first day on Cynofrax. The words he once couldn't define fit perfectly in the rhythm of the anthem.

"That's... almost too serendipitous," Miles said as he figured this out. "It can't be some destiny thing, right?"

Veralis heard Miles out on his discovery, and told him what she could figure. "I don't have a clue how you knew those words. They're ancient and powerful, in the language of Old Cynofrax. Before the Vulpians of today came along, the Old Cynofraxians were our ancestors. There were days when the words they spoke could shake the very foundations of worlds. Everything they said in that primal tongue seemed to carry so much more weight than their letters alone, and not even they could truly understand why. Their words just seemed... beyond definition, even to themselves, but they decided that the universe didn't need to be solved, and not every question needed an answer. Not that it *shouldn't* be, or *must never* be, just that whatever happened was to happen.”

Miles thought about that. Whatever happened was to happen. An odd similarity to how he felt, with a few finer details removed. Though Miles figured that some things could be just fine existing in mystery, he wasn't a pushover. If there was an answer needed, there wouldn't be much that could stop him aside from death itself.

“Proximity alert,” Techbooth stated to cut the philosophizing.

CHAPTER THE TWELFTH

Veralis opened the door to her home, and Arakai, the Vulpian from when Miles first came to Cynofrax stood there. "I figured it would be a good idea to see how Radien was doing, considering the waves he's been making after a relatively short time."

Miles headed up to Arakai, who wasn't in his armor this time, just some casual clothes for the day-to-day on Cynofrax. "I hope that landing didn't give you too much trouble upstairs, it seems to be a big deal, those Plains of the Stars."

"No one upstairs needed to know, since it was resolved without incident," Arakai assured. "And I think you might like to know that some of the counselors at Alindros Parliament are considering granting you a homestead on Cynofrax in observance of what you've done for us all in such short a time."

Miles perked up at this, both shocked and excited. "Really? Then I suppose I can stop freeloading from Veralis, here."

"Hey, it's not freeloading if I offered!"

Miles half-nodded "Right. Either way, I'd be a fool to not accept it if it goes through."

"Smart man. Technically it's only in consideration, but between you and I, that's only because they haven't written it down yet," Arakai finished with an ear twitch, which acted as a wink for Vulpians.

"Well, thanks for the heads-up, Arakai."

Arakai took his leave, and Miles just stood in awe. "I mean... when The Aura makes sure you don't have to sleep, you get a lot done."

A few days later, Miles got the word officially. He now owned a home on Cynofrax, just outside the Alindros city-province in the area known as Sectora Neutros, an area covering at least seventy percent of Cynofrax's landmass. Essentially, this huge swathe of land consisting of self-governed towns and cities that weren't part of a nation-state, but their allegiance remained to the planet as a whole. Alindros's Parliament commissioned and built the home for Miles, to honor his defeat of Avanchenvaldr, and the saving of Hulae, and simply handed the keys to him, so to speak. It wasn't a physical key that opened the door, just advanced biometrics. Miles moved Techbooth and the tools he had from running the Fourteen Werewolves to this new base of his, and told Veralis she was welcome whenever she wished. Veralis, of course, insisted on keeping the Holographic Arena. But since Miles had the Keystone Forge and could make a new one, he agreed.

It took a little under a week to finish the moving process. The house wasn't huge, but Miles had no need of a huge house. Certainly could be a party house, though, complete with a basement for lair purposes. As days passed, and soon weeks, Miles began to feel uneasy at how nothing else had happened that needed his attention, even with his faith that the universe and its peoples could handle themselves and their own matters. Even so...

The device he carried like his phone was basically all in one, with energy scanner as well as communications, and a few other bells and whistles, but it pinged all the same.

"Go on?"

"Interesting greeting, but I get it," Jaden's voice said as her image appeared in video. "You should come to Laksor, I've discovered something that might interest you."

<TODAY I SAVE MYSELF>

Miles took his ship this time, The Aura Runner. He had learned recently that personal energy-based teleports aren't difficult to track, and some planets were less than fond of random individuals appearing out of nowhere. A social faux pas, as it were. It was generally rude to just warp from planet to planet like he had been for the past while. While in warp, Miles found himself humming to himself, but it was not hums that made the random notes of general musical sense.

"Borf borf borf... borf borf Borf, Borf borf Borf, borfa-borf borf Borf... Borf borf Borf... BORF BORF! BORF BORF BOOOOOOORF!"

This continued for some time, Miles simply 'borfing' in song, when he faintly heard Jaden's voice on his comm-link.

"I mean, that's actually pretty good, not sure how he figured it."

"Fuck." Miles realized that he never actually hung up.

"I swear, if I didn't know that you were human, I'd swear you sound exactly like a Death Worlder, ridiculousness when alone and all." She was referring to Raon-Arashal's Death World Vulpians, of course.

The rest of the trip was in silence, even after Miles ended the transmission. Upon arriving on Laksor, someone was on the platform, but they seemed... off.

Miles took another look at the Laksorian, and focused. His eyes turned a golden glow, and he saw a new sheen over reality, and the unmistakable dark red energy that emanated from the Demon, despite the admittedly very well-done disguise.

"Not this time," Miles muttered to himself as he reached for the cutlass on his hip.

"Hold, Radien!" Jaden approached from behind. "That isn't what you believe!"

"I know, that's why I'm gonna end the son of a—"

"No, Radien! Take another look!"

Miles focused again at the Demon, who somehow hadn't noticed them yet. A further look into its power, as it were, and he saw that it had no connection to Hell, as if it had been either released from servitude to the Dark Six, or escaped. "What in all the realms…"

"I needed a test subject for the GAMA. And I found one. I figured out how not just to change his form, but who he was as a creature. It's not just that he doesn't remember being a Demon, but more that those very parts of his life have been deleted from his consciousness. They've ceased to have ever existed."

"The GAMA device was for rewriting genomes, not entire minds!"

"Correction: I told you to get parts for the genomic part of the puzzle. I procured the rest that this needed."

Miles looked to Jaden, and the new Laksorian, who finally figured out that there were some people here. "Oh, hey Jaden!" He waved casually. Miles was not convinced, even if it wasn't obvious in his expression.

"Hi, Erik!" Jaden waved back. "Whatever Demon he used to be, he's not anymore. Most Demons don't actually even have names, only the ones who do something impressive," she whispered.

Jaden walked over to Erik, handing him a small data chip. Currency drive of some kind, then instructing him to get himself something nice to eat. She then took Miles to her laboratory.

"I've no doubt you want every proof in all the universe that this worked," she explained, pulling up audio logs and video tests, as well as written reports on her computer setup. "I captured him on the outskirts of Nagatzul City, Redaria Omega. Take a look at his own testimony."

The video played of a Demon scout restrained to a table, but not nearly as much as was likely needed. "Context: According to this scout's testimony on capture, he dissents the Dark Six, as well as their mission to conquer all reality," Jaden said to the camera, and the Demon nodded.

"I'm not the only one, either. In fact, there are

many Rogue Demons scattered across Hell, some even in this universe. The problem with us is that we very much go all or nothing on our cause. Either a Demon loves nothing more than to kill in their master's name, or they denounce it all and call their 'masters' ridiculous."

"And why don't the Dark Six simply crush those kinds of Demons?" Jaden asked.

"Normally they do. Very few of us get away for any amount of time, let alone escape to your universe. But much like how my kin batter at the walls of your worlds so much that someone eventually breaks through, the same can be said of Rogue Demons. Many rise and quickly fall, almost all of them do. But every now and again, one of them succeeds in running away, just wanting to live beyond this ridiculous forever war the Dark Six rage."

Jaden scribbled some notes in the video feed as the Demon continued.

"The problem is that I can still be tracked by my brethren. I still have a trace to the Dark Six, a trace that can be followed. If my former comrades find me, they'd honestly be more interested in killing me as painfully as possible than killing you and anyone else in their way. But they'd still do it."

"Undoubtedly. So why did you seek me out, and get captured as a result?"

"I heard rumors of your work. Genome Hacking. The ability to change a creature at the most primordial level, and I saw a chance to leave that life behind, truly."

"It can't remove that trace you were talking about though, nor can it change that you would have been a Demon at some point."

"Not yet," the Demon responded, breaking the restraints that bound him to his chair. Jaden jumped up and grabbed an Ion pistol from nearby, pointing it at him with no falter. The Demon seemed to grab something from the air, like it was hidden just outside of visibility, and soon a strange apparatus formed itself in his claws, which he then set down upon the table.

"This can rewrite the consciousness of the willing," he explained. "Operating on consent, it can delete parts of one's own mind, and replace them. I give you my permission to remove all my memories and associations with my time as... this. To make me a new being, a better being."

The video ended, and Miles looked at Jaden again.

"I tested the device, scanned it, everything. It was exactly what he said it was. I was able to program it to make him a Laksorian in body, mind, and spirit after I put it on the GAMA. And though he still had Demonic energy about him... there was no trace to the Dark Six. That chain that meant he could be tracked and bound to their will was gone."

Miles stood, rubbing his chin, trying to figure out just how this was too good to be true. It certainly sounded like it was. "It sounds too good to be true, and I hope you've thought that as well at some point." Jaden nodded when he finally spoke. "I don't think this can be used on the Demons as a whole. Like you said, a subject needs to be willing, borderline wanting for this to work. But I suppose… if more Rogue Demons show up, seeking their flight from the Dark Six, this could very well be used. Get all the information they have, then hit 'em with this."

"My plan exactly," Jaden affirmed. "I'll keep tweaking it, refining the process. Perhaps something more can come of this."

"Admirable ambition, but we might just need to take this miracle at face value."

A few moments passed in silence, and Miles flicked at a few holographic screens, slightly bored now that the conversation was finished. "Was there anything else you needed?"

"I should honestly be asking you that, seeing as I've yet to repay you for getting me the parts I needed for this thing," Jaden replied. "The Bloodstream Accelerant Module trick was a stroke of genius. Almost on my level, but I probably shouldn't brag."

"I tend to avoid tooting my own horn altogether," Miles said with a slight nod. "But I will not forget the next time I need a quick favor."

"What do you need now?" Jaden asked, sitting up on a nearby table. "What could you use at this moment?"

"I'm not sure," Miles answered. "Give someone all the options in the world, and they'll never be able to decide, I suppose." He looked towards the middle distance, like he was trying to piece together a puzzle in his head of his own making. "I... I genuinely don't know. That's so odd. I mean, I know often that I don't know the answer to a question, but that feeling, that understanding that I truly don't know... It's almost harrowing."

"Well, make sure I'm the second to know when you learn it, given that you'll be the first."

Miles nodded, and took his leave, heading back to Cynofrax, and his home outside Alindros. Well, it was actually a pretty good distance from the capital, the closest settlement in fact was a city called Independence. It was mostly inhabited by a mechanical people known as the Ascendant, called such from having ascended to sentience as a species long ago. In fact, Ascendant referred to any mechanical creature who learned how to be sentient. Like other species, they tended to come in all shapes and sizes.

One of Miles's friends he made in the city was called Bringer, who worked at one of the taverns as a bartender. Some Ascendant circles tended to name themselves by pointing at a word at random from a dictionary, which was how the first ones got about it.

"It would be odd for someone like you, I suppose," Bringer finished his point. He and Miles were discussing the outing on Laksor, but Miles omitted the Demon part. "Your story is one that would give yourself great conflict. Stuck as you were, suddenly now it all opens up like you just finished the tutorial of an open-world game? That would confuse anyone of any species on a rather base level."

"It also seems really odd, that... everyone seems to talk like me, right? Not just speaking my language, but talking like me. The way I speak and order my words and such, there's no way every person has that idiolect as well!"

"Well, that would actually be The Aura for you. The universal understanding and such, it doesn't just tell you the words someone's saying. The power is intuitive. It knows what you need to hear to understand the message, and ensures you do. The way you're talking sounds much like mine. It's why we seem to have become friends this quickly. Our words are almost the same, and the only rift would be made by differences and disagreements in morals."

"And what do you hear when you speak and listen?"

Bringer was quick to answer. "Words I understand, in the way I need in order to understand them. What does it matter exactly how I speak to myself, or how exactly I hear you speak to me? You say something, and I hear exactly what you mean. I say something, and you get the same."

"Well, that's real fuckin' helpful."

Bringer laughed, pouring Miles a new pint. "I know."

A moment passed, and Bringer leaned himself against his side of the counter a bit. "I once tried to figure it all out, like you're doing right now. What really are the words he's saying? What is really the message she's trying to tell me? But I've also learned that languages are gods-damned unbelievable messes. Yeah, I could take those actual words and figure out what they were defined as, but that's exactly how misinterpretation happens. That's the literal process to incite it. You use The Aura, I use algorithms embedded in my programming. It gets the job done. Yours probably better than mine, but does that really matter? It works."

Miles took a decent drink from his glass.

"There's plenty of mysteries around that need

solving. Enough matters that demand attention to occupy any of us for a thousand of our lifetimes before we'd get anywhere near to where this sits on the priorities. Hell, by the time we were ready to get to it, a whole new list of better shit to do would create itself. I'd rather repair a bridge when it falters than see if I can tack on extra planks for no real reason. I might be able to build a whole new bridge with all the wood I use to absolutely secure a natural one that has lasted for centuries, and will for millenia more," Bringer continued, almost solemnly.

"Gods, imagine spending that kind of time to preemptively fix what isn't broken by any means," Miles retorted.

"Preemptive is just a polite word for unprovoked."

CHAPTER THE THIRTEENTH

Miles fiddled about with his guitar at the home the Alindros Parliament gave him. Veralis had expressed interest in moving in, as it was a slightly larger home than hers, and Miles saw nothing wrong with the idea, so he had told her she would be welcome.

On his guitar, a riff that made sense musically would be broken up by just plucking at the same string a few times, almost like his mind was wandering as he played, and that wandering would catch up to the rest of him. He soon put the guitar away, and just sat there. The harmonic silence from when he'd sit in those woods on Earth followed. His mind not blank as much as just... unoccupied.

"I still don't believe it all" He finally said to himself

and realized. "I still can't seem to convince myself that indeed, I'm here. I'm still ready to wake up from the nice, comforting dream, serving only to taunt me with visions of what could have been, what should have been…"

Miles sat down at the table, and closed his eyes, soon the harmonic hum of silence filled the air again, and in his mind's eye, he summoned the Effigy. The silent aspect of who Miles would be if he were better.

"Well, I don't have that shop anymore. It was fun while it lasted, though," Miles said aloud, to no response. He just sat there, understanding. More than listening, which is what Miles needed in the Effigy. "I don't actually remember if it was like, a lifelong dream or something neat to have, but I'm leaning more towards the latter these days. But I've finally left Earth for good, and I wouldn't have it any other way."

Grabbing a bottle of light drink, Miles poured two glasses. One for him, and the other for what would be him, but better. The effigy of wisdom would hold whatever Miles poured him, but never actually drank it, given that he was just a projection of Miles's mind, an image of a better kind of person.

Miles sipped from his glass and sighed. "But I still find it hard to believe it's not some cruel dream. Cruel in that it's so nice, and that I'll wake up and have to be back on Earth, with a shitty and stagnant life. Trudging through the roads paved with the same dull grey that is such an infuriatingly capitalistic lockdown on the perception of time and reality itself."

His stronger image listened.

"And as this, this all continues, and I forge such great memories and alliances, I see more and more that I couldn't stand the idea of leaving it all. I'd kill, I'd die if it meant I could go back to this if I learned it was all just conjured. Another nice, comfortable fantasy to pass the time between one maddening trench of stagnation and the next."

His stronger image listened.

"The universe I'm seeing, with so much good to offer, and not even offer, just present, like that's how it's supposed to be... it's just so too good to be true to me. I can't comprehend the idea that the universe is... kind. I can't bring myself to think that the worlds are kind."

His stronger image continued to listen.

"And even now, as I rant of how it can't be real because it's just too nice, I wonder how much it irritates you and the people around me to hear how I, so petty and closed-minded, continue to think like this when it does nothing but disservice to me. How annoyed must everyone be, that despite all they do, I still put walls up for myself because I can't find them naturally?"

His stronger image remained listening.

Miles sighed again, knocking back the drink he had poured. "Wounds that I seem to inflict myself because no one else will. What kind of petty entitlement must I have that even begins to think that's justified?"

His stronger image still listened.

Miles's head hit the table with a thud, before looking back up at his shadow of light, as it were.

"If nothing else, I'm very incurably me," Miles said to himself. "I'm sure I'll figure this out eventually, however it ends up happening. I can't seek it, because it's one of those things that if you actively look for it, it drives the answer further away. As long as the universe continues to let me participate in it, I'll bet that one day, I'll stop worrying about waking up."

Radien poured himself another glass, even though he was going to drink what he had given his effigy as well once this was over.

"One day, I'll figure that this was my waking up."

Miles nodded to his effigy, and closed his eyes. When he opened them again, the being was gone. The image of who he'd be proud to be had vanished, returning to the realm of imagination. He then finished the drinks on the table.

After collecting himself and waiting for the fog in his head and motor functions to clear, Miles took his ship to a planet called Caren'Das, having received a request for investigatory aid from a one Kendro-Dalinor, who identified himself by the rank of Exemplar.

After some research, Miles learned that the Exemplar is an elected position within the Hajivakk people, and every planet with a significant Hajivakk population has an Exemplar, who acts as a beacon of morality for the Haji-Son, setting the example of what it means to live and do well.

Landing on Caren'Das after a several-hour warp, during which he configured the internal layout of The Aura Runner, Miles met with Exemplar Kendro-Dalinor, who was accompanied by a pair of bodyguards.

"Radien, your battle on Hulae is well-known already, and the Haji-Son recognize you as a worthy ally of our people. Which is why I've called upon you to help with a matter here on Caren'Das."

"Your people honor me with such a title as 'worthy ally'," Miles said, bowing his head slightly. "What do you need?"

Kendro-Dalinor escorted Miles to his home, where they discussed an apparent cache of information of great historical significance.

"It was recently revealed that this info-cache existed. We're not sure where exactly, but we know it's on the ruined world of Alabasteron. The information concerns the actions of the Hajivakk people during the

Sentience War of the Fifth Cosmic Era," Kendro-Dalinor explained over a holographic map of the titular ruin.

"I feel like I should know what most of those words meant."

"Fair enough. The entirety of the Fifth Cosmic Era was spent fighting the single bloodiest war in all of time, the Sentience War. Far deadlier than the Demon War long before, tens of trillions of lives were lost during this blood era, and that's an optimistic number. It was fought not between races or peoples, but two ideals answering a single question: 'Can a mechanical species gain sentience?' The Ascendant people had just begun to make themselves known, and the Shard, the race that produced them had zero intent on their recognition, even changing the standard by which sentience is recognized intergalactically to assure it. The war ended on Prismos, when the last of the Shard people made their self-absorbed stand, refusing to admit that their mechanical slaves had learned how to feel, and how to think. Prismos was destroyed, and the Shard became extinct. But the neighboring planet, Alabasteron, became known as the Graveworld after so many battles had been fought there. It was the hub of the military power of the Shard's allies, who agreed with their most vile intolerance of the new species. However, most of the Hajivakk people's involvement in the war had been forgotten by us, until we picked up this ancient signal."

Kendro-Dalinor pressed a button, showing that a transmission was indeed being broadcasted.

"It's the frequency our ancestors used to hide these sorts of 'information arks' for a given amount of time. Someone programmed that cache, billions of years ago, to transmit on this day that the information was here: The Haji-Son account of the Sentience War."

"So, what stops everyone from going down there to grab it?" Miles asked.

"So much hate and anger flowed with the blood that spilled on Alabasteron, that the people who fell cannot seem to cease fighting their battle, even beyond death. Their ancient skeletons still remain, constantly warring with each other, and never finally dying. No one wants to risk going there. Not against a foe you can't kill."

"And why does that mean I have to go down there?"

"You're on the outside. Your species wasn't even single-celled back then, they may hear you out that you are just passing through, and have no desire to get involved."

Miles nodded, making sense of the plan. "Very well. I'll head there, and convince the skeletons to let me have that infocache."

Kendro-Dalinor thanked him, and Miles set the course of The Aura Runner to Alabasteron. Upon entering orbit near one of the rusty cities, he could see that a few hundred miles away, the ancient battle was still being fought, lasers and bullets flying and meeting their mark, but never getting the job done. Miles climbed out of The Aura Runner, having landed it just out of eyeshot of the city, then hiding it with a Temporal Displacement, which desynchronized the ship from the rest of the timeline by a single second, effectively hiding the craft one second in the future.

Miles made his way up to the gate of this city, which despite its decrepit look, was a solidly fortified base. Several skeletons of precursor races eyed him, just as resolutely guarding as they had in life.

"Your business here?" one asked, somehow managing to form a voice from only bones.

"I need to speak to the General, or someone close to that. There's something not far from here I need to pick up, and it's in hot territory."

One nodded to the other, and the gate opened enough for Miles to enter. "Look for the Gilded Fragment Inn. He'll be there."

Miles made his way through, cautiously as he could without looking suspicious, despite being unsure how he could look suspicious to skeletons of people he couldn't even figure what species they used to be.

Finding the Gilded Fragment, Miles walked in and looked for the leader the guards said would be here. Eventually, he sat down next to him at a table.

"My men outside say you're looking for something in hot territory," he started.

"Aye, an information ark at this location." Miles grabbed his scanner, showing the general where the Hajivakk's prize was located.

"Hot territory indeed. I'm not sure how large an escort I can spare."

"I don't need an escort as much as a couple scouts to act as another few sets of eyes, making sure I won't encounter any resistance along the route."

The General nodded, agreeing to lend three scouts to watch the path. Before Miles could even question the strangely cooperative nature of the people he was dealing with, the door to the inn flung open, revealing several skeletal soldiers toting automatic weapons of some make.

"Oh shit, it's Bones Malone and the Spook Troop!" a patron said from afar.

"RATTLE 'EM, BOYS!" the center man shouted, and opened fire. Miles hit the deck, kicking over one of the tables for cover. Then he realized that tables make for shitty cover, but at least he was out of sight. Bullets were flying, and so were the bones of patrons and staff, the General even was caught in the crossfire. Soon, the mangled remains of a bar full of skeletons were all that was left for Miles to behold, before something incredible happened.

The fallen began to reassemble themselves, crunching and cracking back into place, even healing their own fractures. Some started laughing once it was done, and even the assailants weren't immune. Miles poked his head out from behind his table, confused as all hell, and everyone was congratulating each other on a job well done.

"You are owed an explanation for sure," the General said as he popped his own bony arm back into his shoulder. "Follow me."

After entering a back room with some charts and maps, Miles got his explanation.

"Long ago, there were a great number of awful battles that happened on this world due to what we came to know as the Sentience War. We all fought and killed each other. But we wouldn't rest. So many emotions, so much passion, and hate, and anger with what we did and what we stood for... death couldn't keep us from our desire to fight. We thought it was a one-off for a while, and took the miracle as it looked. But we all eventually figured it out: For some reason, we just can't die. But by the time we all knew it and calmed the hell down with what we were fighting over, the universe had moved on, and called Alabasteron a cursed world."

"Why are you still fighting then?"

The General laughed. "We're honestly not, but it sure looks like we are. Now it's just a huge joke, one we have to keep up to fool the rest of the universe. So from a distance and a quick glance, it looks like we're still trying to win a war won billions of years ago, but take a closer look and that ridiculous shit a few minutes back is just the tip of the iceberg on how much irony bleeds from what we do to keep the charade up. Planet of the Ridiculous Shenanigans, that's what Alabasteron has become."

Miles stood there, piecing it together.

"The guy who shouted before they opened fire? He'd been practicing that line for weeks. It was planned, staged, all of it. That's why I could give you those scouts. I'd then immediately call the guys in that area to back off of it for a bit. They'd do it, and find some other insane comedy act to figure out next."

"So why remain on Alabasteron?"

"The universe fought the bloodiest war in history over whether or not a machine could feel feelings. Can you imagine the shitshow that would be if that question became 'can the dead feel feelings'?"

Miles agreed quickly. "Regardless, I still need that Hajivakk information ark."

"Not a problem, just as long as you keep this between us. The rest of the worlds have no need to know that we're as we are now, and honestly? We haven't gotten bored enough yet to try our luck on it."

Eventually shaking off the absurdity, Miles took The Aura Runner to the Hajivakk information ark, and opened it. Both electronic records and physical writings of the species's involvement in the Sentience War, that the Skeletons of Alabasteron had made into such an enormous joke to save face. While on his way back to Caren'Das, Miles studied the records. Apparently, the Haji-Son at the time were one of a couple races that were quick to act against the Shard when they showed their oppressive colors, but they were single most eager. They had known of the Shard's evil for some time, but hadn't the resources to act. As soon as the Vulpians and Redarians at the time made their stance clear, the Hajivakk soon followed, and couldn't wait to stomp some space racists. At least, more so than the others involved.

"Your people will be pleased to know that the Haji-Son were eager to fight the Shard's oppression of the Ascendant species," Miles explained when he returned to Exemplar Kendro-Dalinor.

"I must admit, I was worried for a while that we

had sided with the Shard for an amount of time during the conflict. I'm glad to have been proven wrong of that worry."

"I know what you mean," Miles empathized. "You go looking for information, only to find out it's not the kind you hoped to see, and then you go into a hell of a funk trying to shake off the fact that once indeed, you or people not far from you did the abominable."

A moment passed as Kendro-Dalinor eyed Miles, as if that were too specific of an example to be anything short of a confession.

"But it is one of the few times where one is relieved to be proven wrong," Miles finished.

"Indeed. I trust the restless souls on Alabasteron did not give you too much trouble?"

This was the part where Miles needed to lie. Or hopefully only have to omit the truth.

"It went well, yes. I was able to call myself unaffiliated, and get the information ark without incident."

"They still fight?"

"They still fight."

Thankfully, Kendro-Dalinor did not ask how they fought, or anything else for that matter. Although Miles had gotten some ideas for comedy routines out of what the skeletons of Alabasteron did to 'fight' each other.

CHAPTER THE FOURTEENTH

How long had it actually been since Miles gained his power? This was the question on his mind when the Conclave of Sentience on Turazin contacted him, stating that the humans of Earth had finally figured out where the rest of the universe was hiding. With progress inspired by Miles's battle with Avanchenvaldr, the humans had contacted a Loriken ship passing by the solar system, and now Miles had to testify. He was the catalyst between the people of Earth, and the rest of the peoples in the communicable universe. Miles made his way to Turazin, and waited in the Conclave chambers for the proceeding to follow.

"Did they actually manage to elect a single representative for themselves?" Miles asked, to the nods of a few Conclave members. "I am genuinely surprised."

The door behind him opened, and a man in his mid thirties stepped to the podium next to Miles's designated spot.

"Surely they told you why I'm here, right?" Miles asked.

"Yes, I've been informed. Conrad Stonewall, by the way."

"Miles Radien."

"I don't think there's anyone on Earth who doesn't know your name by now."

Another surprise for Miles, and the meeting began.

"It should be known by all parties that this should not be interpreted as interrogation, or necessarily a test. This is for the purpose of learning as much as possible, the best way to get about this, and future proceedings," Xenidar said. He was the neutral party to ask the questions of Conrad, representing the humans.

"Per prior statement and evidence supplied by Miles Radien, the Humans of Earth have already demonstrated themselves as sentient creatures under The Pillars Three. The Conclave does not question whether or not Humans are sentient. It is already confirmed," Xenidar stated

Conrad nodded, and Xenidar continued. "The

Conclave's first question to the Human representative: Given that the history of your species is known, we do observe that amongst yourselves you have engaged in warfaring methods recognized as morally forbidden and absolutely illegal. These methods mostly are non-discriminatory weapons, such as atomic radiation, vaporous substances, and the use of non-sentient single cell organisms."

"Basically nuclear, gases, and bio-weapons. Stuff you can't point at someone," Miles explained to Conrad, who nodded.

"In order for the Conclave to accept the Humans into the intergalactic community, and for us to aid the peoples of Earth in their technologies and progresses, the Humans must totally renounce the aforementioned methods of warfare. It is understood by the Conclave that combat is sometimes the only option, but there is a difference between combat and depravity."

Conrad looked over at Miles, as if he wanted to make sure he was interpreting things correctly. "Total nuclear disarmament, and agreeing to never use nukes, gas, or biological warfare again as weapons."

"I'm afraid I can only speak for myself when I say I am absolutely in favor of the Conclave's policies, but I worry what will happen when some of the less than moral types on Earth inevitably resist this," Conrad said to the Conclave.

"Do explain," a Taigron requested.

"Humans are, unfortunately, a heavily divisible race. I fear that some people on Earth will see the disarmament you want as a sign of weakness on their part, and will inevitably do something completely stupid. I truly do not care what would happen to them personally at that point, but my worry instead is for everyone else who may be judged alongside them for association."

"These are my thoughts as well, it should be known," Miles added. "I've little doubt that there will be humans who both want nothing more than to abide by the Conclave's wishes, and others who will see this as an insult. I hope that some kind of accord can be reached that allows the humans who do want what the Conclave wants, can be allowed into the universe, as it were."

"And what do you propose be done about the humans who would cling to their abominable weapons?" a familiar Hykentiu asked. It was Dorg.

"They have to remain on Earth until they quit throwing temper tantrums, I'd imagine."

Conrad nodded at this, clearly this was a better idea than he had initially.

"Radien, you are likely the person the Conclave trusts the most on this matter, so this decision falls to you. Should the Humans be allowed into the community that is this grand universe?" Xenidar said. The Conclave's members were unsure of themselves in regards to the Humans, given that Miles was the only one they knew, whose opinion of them was mixed, to say the least.

Miles thought to himself for a moment. It felt like a long moment, but it likely wasn't.

"By the guidelines I have suggested, yes. The individual humans who agree by the Conclave's requirements should be granted all the rights of recognized species. The rest stay on Earth until they mature, so to speak. I ask that a planet that can support humans be designated for them to settle on, and that the Conclave allocate as much resources as necessary to make this work right. If my battle with Avanchenvaldr did make a difference, I'm willing to take this chance."

Miles looked to Conrad, who nodded.

"It is settled then. As many ships as needed, with as much supply as comfortable will be used to aid in this process and ensure that it is done both correctly, and speedily. We have already found a planet that is habitable by human standards, and currently is uncolonized."

Conrad seemed surprised by this until Miles explained. "They've actually got a database of planets that have been set aside for the purpose of giving them to newly recognized species."

"That's incredible!" Conrad said. "I promise you, Conclave, we will not forget this graciousness! On my life, I will make sure we don't let you down!"

"Then the meeting is adjourned," Xenidar stated, and Conrad left excitedly. Miles waited until the doors closed behind him to speak.

"I know that's a big promise from him, but don't hold either him or the Humans as a whole to it as hard as you might for me. You're going to be giving a lot of people a second chance, or rather, a first chance that they never got for the longest time. There's gonna be people with choices and options they didn't even know were capable of existing. It's gonna be rough for the first while, and I don't mean rough as in bad… I mean more as in… tentative. Confusing. Like baby steps."

"Yeah, I getcha," Xenidar said, back in his regular informal upbeat. "This isn't the first time the Conclave has had a 'trouble race' to help out. They know what they're doing. Trust me if not them on that."

When Miles returned to his home on Cynofrax, he made himself some beef soup. Or rather, the local beef equivalent soup. But what he did next was to turn most of the lights in the house off, leaving only the night sky outside and a dimmed light from the next room over as the light sources. He then proceeded to eat that soup in the darkness, and he felt a euphoria he couldn't quite give a name to, but it certainly was good. To eat soup alone, in the darkness of a large, empty house.

A knock on his door ended the aloofness of the matter. Veralis had arrived with some of her stuff, given that she was moving in. She was a little confused at the scene that she had interrupted.

"Are you just eating soup in the darkness?" she asked.

"Lemme tell you something, Veralis. Eating soup alone in the darkness evokes an emotion that I really don't have a name for, but it's one of the best damn ones I get."

She was still rather confused. "So uh... should I hold off on this for a bit?"

"No, you're fine. Besides, I've been doing this since I was given this house. One interruption isn't going to ruin me."

Veralis unpacked the things she'd brought over, including the Holographic Arena Projector, which they set up in an appropriate room. After a quick test run to make sure it was working, Miles went back to the table to finish that soup, albeit neither alone or in the darkness. Veralis joined Miles at the table, eyeing him as if she couldn't figure something out about how he worked.

"Need something?" Miles asked.

"It's just... The way you've adapted to The Aura, the things you've already done for the worlds, that takes a particular kind of person. But the thing is, you were born on a planet with no Fonts, no means of fulfilling yourself in any way. It's a wonder you didn't turn catatonic on such a purgatory world."

"Who's to say I didn't?" Miles commented. "I still feel like I am sometimes. Earth wasn't just the kind of place to drive you nuts. It's the kind of place that takes you beyond insanity, to when screaming itself becomes silent because after all that time of all that bullshit and madness, it tunes itself out. You get so mad that you no longer feel anything, like when an ear-splitting screech becomes high-pitched enough to be outside your hearing range."

Veralis grabbed some soup of her own from the pot.

"And I wonder if... that level of anger will go back down to an audible level, if that makes any sense. With finally my escape from Earth and its confines, will I suddenly find myself outwardly insane again now that the hate can die down, back into that hearing range?"

"I more believe that your silent catatonia has overloaded and died altogether," Veralis postulated. "You came to Cynofrax, and had your first nights on a planet that wasn't Earth. I'm willing to think that would've caused that nonsensical confusion to become too much to even continue surviving. And with already the screech beyond your hearing range, as you put it, the popping of that overfilled balloon wasn't even hearable."

Miles half-nodded, in a way that showed he hoped she was right.

Eventually, Veralis took her leave, and Miles was once again eating soup alone in the darkness. One does not know nirvana-level solitude until they have eaten soup, alone, in the darkness. He sat there for a while, pondering this. He closed his eyes.

He heard the harmonic hum of the sound of silence.

"I never actually could really get the best of looks at you," Miles said as he opened his eyes. "I'd always understand that you were here, even when I couldn't *see* you physically. But now I can. I guess The Aura's giving you a little boost into my visual cortex."

He had once again summoned his wiser effigy to sit with him as he ate soup in the darkness. "Do you think... there's gonna be some kind of big trial? I honestly wonder, will my life in this new universe consist entirely of the odd skirmish here and there, helping out where I can? Or am I gonna fight a proper battle, against a real foe?"

Miles thought for a moment. "Those were not the right words. I know that for sure. I just don't know what the right words are. Although, it is nice that you're still here. There's a lot of things I left behind on Earth that definitely need to stay behind. I think you're the one thing I'm happy to have taken with me."

Miles nodded, and closed his eyes, 'dismissing' the effigy once again.

But out of nowhere, Miles felt a jolt through the earth, like something had slammed against the ground with sudden and potent force. He whipped around in his chair, but saw the field outside his home consumed in a swirling crimson storm, this house of his in its eye. Everything pulled itself apart around him, the roof, the walls, the table, even that bowl of soup. The grass tore away from the dirt, and the dirt tore away from the stone. A dark figure emerged from the whirling walls of the storm, encased in a deep red glow. Miles thrust his hand out to fire a bolt, but only a few sparks that quickly fizzled out were all he created.

"Dammit, no!" Miles yelled, attempting to fire again and again, to no avail. The figure approached loomingly, and when Miles took a few steps back, the shadowy being seemed to move forward in his vision beyond its footsteps, a lurching doom that did not cease, the manifest of a timer running out.

Miles cursed and charged the figure, striking at it with a flurry of trained punches and kicks, but the being was not harmed. The strikes didn't even make this being's cursed flesh move, and Miles was only pushed back by his strikes, like he was trying to kick through a wall of solid steel. The being did not budge to his assault.

It threw a strike of its own, swinging its arm at Miles like it was going to swat him away. Miles put up his arms to block it, but this seemingly inconsequential move utterly overpowered him, and Miles was sent careening through the air and onto the ground. Miles yelled in frustration, still trying to fire a few bolts, but now the sparks were barely fizzles. The being stood before him, and turned its back to him. Miles unleashed hell with hands and feet, hitting every weak point on the body, but the being was as unmoving as ever. Miles could not harm it. He tried to put his knee into its spine, but he didn't pull it down into his knee as much as lifted himself up on it, only for nothing of use to happen. Miles kicked at the crease in the back of its legs, but his foot was pushed back like he just tried to move a skyscraper with a flick. He climbed this creature, and drove his elbow down on top of its head, several times, screaming in rage, but nothing happened. The creature reached up and grabbed him, tossing him aside like he was a disobedient fool.

The being stared at him with piercing red eyes,

evil darker than the storm around them was harsh. Then, it all stopped. Miles still lay on the ground, but everything faded. The being faded, the storm faded, and his home faded back into reality. The bowl of soup was still on the table, undisturbed as if Miles had simply fallen out of his chair.

"That damn nightmare should be gone!" Miles growled.

He came to The Aura Prism to discuss this dark vision. The Effigy couldn't help him on this, he needed answers.

"And this is not the first time you have been haunted by this vision?" The Prism asked after Miles told his story.

"No, far from it," Miles said solemnly. "I've even had a name for it for years: The Opponent Unbeatable. No matter what I do, no matter where I strike, stab or shoot, or anything, this dark foe simply cannot be harmed by me. And it knows. It barely tries to stop me from... wailing on it! I do everything I know how, and it gives me nothing! I can't stop this damned thing!"

Miles sighed and sat down at the peak of The Mountain. "And with The Aura... I thought that nightmare was over! I thought that vision should fade and become a thing of the past, a twisted machination of a mind that no longer needed to think that way!"

A moment passed.

"Maybe there's been some Demon haunting me on Earth that just now figured out I'm on Cynofrax? Maybe we can run some trace on this thing's energy? It might still be there since it's that recent, right?"

"I truly wish I could tell you yes, Radien," The Prism said with an ached tone. "I do wish I could say that a Demon does just haunt you. But this is unfortunately a spawn of your mind, indeed a machination of one that should never have had to think that way."

Miles sighed again, knowingly. He knew there was no way this was anything other than him. "Yeah... It's not even that this thing is scary, you know? All that parts that make it up, the storm, the being, the physical appearance of it all isn't a scary thing. It does not scare me the look of what I beheld. It's the message. It's what it stands for, and tells me, and makes me understand. Hell, I can hear already all those token voices from everyone else all 'face your fears!' or 'stand up to it!' and the like, but this isn't something you can face like you'd face a fear of heights by going into like, a skyscraper or some shit! This isn't a fear of what is or was! It's a dread of how it could go so horribly wrong! I mean, I can't even call it a fear proper because I don't feel the emotion of fear with this, and I know that!"

Miles let out an audible 'ugh,' and flopped

backwards onto the ground.

"I would ask why you have not told Veralis, Jarrek, Arakai or Miirkae of this torment, but I already understand. And no, it's not because I can read your mind. It's because I understand how someone like you works," The Prism said after almost a full minute of silence.

"Aye," Miles acknowledged. "People can misinterpret, people can fail to understand. But powers don't lie. The Aura isn't something that can lie. It's a power, a fact of the universe. It can't have an ulterior motive or a 'different experience' in the traditional sense."

"You understand me to not be a person?"

"I understand you to be what I need for this, and what I need is decidedly *not* a person."

"Then I suppose that is a compliment here."

"In this sense, absolutely."

Another moment of silence.

"I've said it before, Radien," the Prism iterated. "You spent way too much time on a planet you didn't belong to. When you say 'people,' you think of a human person who, if misinterpretation was a profession, they'd be champion of the universe."

"Depending on who you ask, it *is* a profession on Earth."

"Regardless, you hear the word 'people' and can't help but think of humanity. That ridiculous, word-twisting lot who almost seem to like taking the piss in direct proportion to how much they need to not do that at a given moment. I know you don't see all your allies like that, but I do know you keep yourself vigilant, just to make sure things work. Or rather, make sure things at least don't utterly fail to work."

"Everyone has plenty on their table to worry about, this is a trivial matter. It concerns only myself and my own little bad dream. Veralis has a bar to run nowadays, she actually manages that place in Kaldres-Viane. Arakai's Arch-Militant of the Cynofrax Militarium now, Jarrek has Redaria's own military to command, Miirkae has his Conclave business, Jaden's got her research, which she's done surprisingly miraculously on... I would gladly consider this something that can wait for them to deal with their own business taking place within physical reality." Miles even considered checking in on Jaden as he recalled these details.

"I have no doubt you would," The Prism affirmed.

"If this becomes a physical reality issue, it will without hesitation be brought to their attention, with all the information I have so that we may combat it, even if I can't figure out how myself."

The Prism remained silent on this. Not out of

doubt or judgment, but because there was nothing more that could be said without losing the point. Miles stood up finally.

"This helped, Prism," Miles said. "Thanks."

"Needed someone to listen but not advise?"

"Not really. It's not that I needed someone to listen, or someone to affirm me, but just... I needed to speak with The Aura Prism on this matter."

"I think I get it..." The Prism hesitantly noted.

"You only think so?"

"Radien, I do sincerely hope you don't think I am omniscient. If I knew everything, the universe would simply be no fun. There'd be no reason to watch over it, no purpose in participating in the experience of reality."

Miles nodded. "I might use that one someday."

It was another few days before anything new came to his attention, but Miles remained vigilant in this downtime all the same. The return of his vision of the Opponent Unbeatable shook him, the very idea that it could still come to him after all he's done, and all he's proven himself to be to himself...

Either way, Miles took his ship to the planet of Bol'Drakkin, homeworld of one of the genetic castes of the Draconian species. Specifically, the Bol'Drakkin Genetic Caste, as one might expect given that this was their homeworld. Regardless, the Bol'Drakkin Draconians were likely what Melaqros was.

Miles was to meet with someone by the name of Lakarium the Brightblade, a patriarch of the Jurovendr Battle Brothers, one of the prominent families on Bol'Drakkin, but not in the traditional sense. More in the sense of a family that one chooses to call themselves a part of. Miles met with Lakarium, one of their warrior-trainers, and was led to a private ring, normally meant for testing.

"Though I normally use this for testing purposes, it serves well as a place for private discussion," Lakarium established. "I'll cut to what you need to know: I'm not sure I'm comfortable with your support of your Human kin entering the wider universe."

"Neither am I," Miles said. "It's a risk for sure, and I've little doubt I will question myself many times before the result is realized."

"Sooner than you might think," Lakarium commented, sliding a table in, where he placed a dossier folder. "There's already a human gang on Bol'Drakkin making waves in the way of, how might you say it, 'shitting things the fuck up'."

Worried, Miles flipped through the folder, seeing that hundreds of Human colonists on Bol'Drakkin had been less than stellar by the laws of the Draconian people. Several assaults, along with goading citizens into fights only to disparage them for accepting the clear challenge. A few accounts of disorderly conduct-like regard, and it was clear there wouldn't be much time between now and when someone did something particularly egregious.

"I wonder if these guys are even supposed to be off Earth," Miles questioned. "The Conclave made it clear that people would have to prove themselves of good moral before entering the wider universe... but the problem is that humans can be very good liars when they want to get something done that a truthful answer can't"

Miles continued looking through the folder, becoming progressively more angered as the offenses became more heinous.

"I suppose this also is a test that I might better know you," Lakarium added. "After your battle at Hulae, I figured I needed to meet you at some point."

Miles was more concentrated on how much the humans on Bol'Drakkin were insulting their welcome. "I'd definitely end these guys if it weren't for how early it is in their universe career of sorts. I just know what kind of problems it would cause... but that said, I certainly can make sure they won't be harassing people again if they want to continue living."

Lakarium nodded as Miles took his leave,

grabbing the folder to make sure he remembered who he was after. It turned out they weren't difficult to track, as some locals had been keeping tabs on where they were at any given point, so as to let people know where to avoid. A group of six humans walked down an empty sidewalk, laughing degradingly and making ridiculous comments, mostly around how scared the locals seemed to be of them.

"I mean, look at this shit! The dumbass lizards can't fuckin' stand up to us! At all!" one of them shouted out in the open, clearly intending to goad someone into a fight. Miles rounded the corner and faced towards them.

"Ey, ey! There's one of us!" another said as he pointed at Miles. "Ey, you know where they all went? Can't stand the idea of getting on our bad side, am I right?" He held out his hand, expecting a high-five.

"I think they just consider you lot not even worth their time," Miles commented.

The group of humans seemed confused at this, and one of the women in the group scoffed. "So, they just run away? You ask me, I'd say they'd have to put a lot of time into planning how to run away!" The rest laughed with that.

Miles sighed. He knew how this had to go, and also how he'd prefer to run things.

"There's not a word I can say that will convince

you to believe otherwise," Miles said. "So instead I'm going to take direct action."

Before any of the group could even let out a chuckle at the comment, six bolts of The Aura's energy flew towards the group, stopping themselves just beneath each of their throats.

"If I had things my way, these bolts would not stop. They'd pass straight through you and loop back around to punch through your chest as well. Unfortunately, as indeed 'one of you,' I understand that shitwits like you will only grow in number until I inevitably have to put all of you down, or at least get every species in the galaxy to help me with it."

The bolts fizzled out with a wave of Miles's hand, and the humans just stood there. Miles could feel them wanting to shout some slur, yell some profanity or curse. He could taste their want to call him a sympathizer for what they would undoubtedly call 'sub-human,' because to a human, all things other than themselves are beneath them. But they knew they could not hope to win this fight.

"If I hear of you or any other human on this or any planet causing this kind of trouble again, flaunting your dicks about thinking you're so much better than everyone else because you're *you* and you're *just that special*, you will all become the dirt I walk on. That will be my insult to you. *You will be proven the lesser that you call everyone that isn't you."*

A moment passed. "Now get lost, and don't let yourself be found," Miles spat, and the hoodlums quickly shuffled away. They didn't run, they'd never let their pride be that damaged.

Though it felt nice overall to give hell to the kinds of Humans Miles would've killed on Earth, he cringed slightly once they were out of sight. He definitely could've had a better speech and even target for his bolts to stop right before. At least, ones that didn't make him look like the kind of person you might accidentally cut yourself on their edginess if you listened to them for too long.

CHAPTER THE FIFTEENTH

Miles sat in his home, once again eating soup in the darkness. Over the past few weeks, strange incidents had been occurring with Humans that had been allowed into the wider universe. Not even necessarily evil, but strange. Some reported a sudden spike in intelligence, such as one Human on Sharaeine, homeworld of the Loriken species, who suddenly invented an 'auto-smelter' device, capable of sorting scrap metals and alloys into their individual elements, a process that while it had been done, it needed an enormous industrial machine. But a Human apparently found a way to make a sort of 'desktop' version, and even out of reasonably affordable materials. Conversely, another Human on the Taigron-controlled planet of Kayvas-Sorven had gone catatonic, exiling himself to a cave on the planet, and detonating an explosive charge at its entrance, sealing himself in. His last words were allegedly. *"Exilon cora, Malmaxus denira!"* before the cave-in.

The reaction from other species had been concern far more than malice. Even many other Humans agreed that there was something going on, something fundamentally altering the behavior of the species. Miles had his suspicions that the Dark Six were involved, but their telltale energy was not present on any Human, let alone the affected ones, whether good or bad.

"It is also possible that natural selection is finally doing its job," Miles said to himself after finishing the soup he had been eating in the darkness. He remained at the table, trying to decide what was next. It was still odd to be able to just do something he wanted to. It likely would never stop being odd that he had a whole universe of whatever he chose to do. Opting to train in the Holographic Arena some, he looked at the cutlass that he had become very familiar with. Novasteel, the metal was called. Apparently, when a star went supernova, there was a point between the explosion itself and the formation of a Neutron Star where the material was manipulable. The metal produced would have the sheer durability of a Neutron Star's material, but without the incredible density that would likely have his sword weigh as much as an average moon. Hunderfold simply referred to the number of times the metal had been folded. Exactly one hundred, and this made it capable of permanently killing Demons. No one was sure why this was the number, let alone why any more would negate this effect. But it worked, and that's what mattered.

But while this blade was impressive, it lacked a certain... flair, as it were. But flair may not have been the right word for it. It didn't really fit him. The metal looked like a rainbow puked on it, with that gasoline-like texture a metal can get after too intense an acid wash that tried and failed to bring out some color. It was nice at first, but it was getting old to look at. The hilt's handle itself didn't really scream his style, either. A sort of light polymer that while it worked and worked well, there had to be something better. The thing was translucent, and something about that just made him inherently uncomfortable. Probably the fact it looked like a plastic handle. The tools in his workshop certainly could help with a makeover for this thing. After 3D-scanning the cutlass into the Phase-Forge's software, he toyed a bit with what he could do to improve it. To start, he looked at the hilt assembly. The Phase-Forge could remove the polymer handle around the tang, and replace it with a durable wood of some kind. After several hours more than what would normally be healthy, Miles had finally chosen to use a species called Belariq Ironwood, apparently highly valued in small-scale woodworking such as pens, keepsake boxes, and hilts. The wood was incredibly tough, but useless in construction due to making for very brittle construction material. But it was perfect for pen blanks and the like.

With that settled, something had to be done about the blade itself. This took a lot less time to figure out, as it was possible for the Phase-Forge to electroplate the sword with Carbon, which would render it jet-black in coloration, and no loss of durability. But speaking of durability, Miles learned of an interesting compound called Red Dust, typically used in projectile weapons. It was an enhancement compound that was used in place of gunpowder for kinetic projectile launchers (or "traditional firearms", if you prefer) and worked better as an accelerant. In laser weapons, lacing the refractor prisms with Red Dust would amplify the beam's power. Plasma would burn hotter, and energy weapons would get a bit more kick. But could Red Dust be used to enhance a sword?

Searching the Galus-Net, there were mixed accounts. Some said it was possible, others denied it entirely. But the closest thing to what Miles sought was a theory on creating a variant of Red Dust that could be bound into the metal of a sword as a sort of 'ultimate sword oil,' which would allow the blade to retain its edge for eons, and even protect it from rust for as long. The theory was promisingly solid, and it looked like the only thing it was missing was actually just a way to bind it to the metal. A way like a Phase-Forge, which a personal-use version hadn't been created yet. It seemed a little too convenient, but within a few days, Miles had his Red Dust for the sword.

The final personal touch was to laser-etch some runes into the sword as the final step, and use the remaining Red Dust as a paint of sorts to make the Elder Futhark glow. Berkanan, Othila, Raido, Fehu upon both sides of the forte, just before the bell. With everything punched into the Phase-Forge and ready to go, the cutlass soon finally had its visual update, one might say. The edge itself glowed with the solid red of the runes on the forte. Not a bright or deep red, but a solid red indeed.

There it was, the Borfblade, as Miles addressed it. This was definitely a weapon he could be proud to have associated with him. Not a cowardly gun, not a ridiculously-designed impractical sword. But this. Maybe there'd be more to it in time, if he could think of it. But right now, *this* was his sword. As much as he had firearms, namely the AZP-621 pistol and the Collapse Rifle, he'd definitely choose this first. Those weapons would probably only come in battles with galaxies and more at stake. That aside, the Borfblade was the weapon he could be proud of.

While he consulted the makeover of his sword, Jaden made her own findings known to Miles. Apparently the human genome acted almost perfectly as a baseplate for many other life forms, including Demons. Even though she already had rewritten a willing Demon's consciousness, the dark power half-woven into the human DNA sequence showed primordial links to Demonic genomes beyond consciousness itself. A solid idea for sure, but Miles insisted that only the consciousness of willing Demons be turned Laksorian, as Jaden made it clear that the template of her native species was the easiest to turn another creature into. There just didn't be wanted the risk of a Demon overriding the process, and turning the whole plan into splinters of what was once a good idea.

Jaden continued her research, and Miles continued his overall quest to better understand himself, albeit interrupted by near entire days worth of pondering. But one could easily call that part of Miles's goal, especially if you were the kind of person who could make a high school English teacher shudder at your overanalysis of symbolism.

Eventually, Jaden contacted Miles directly.

"If you've got a moment, Radien, you might be interested in what I'm sending your way right now."

With nothing better to do, let alone much at all, Miles was more than willing to hear her out.

"I assume you aren't familiar with the mythical text known as the Manifest of Apocalypse, so along with the information pertinent, I've attached a brief summary of what you need to know about it."

Even with the amount of time Miles had spent traveling, he hadn't heard of the Manifest of Apocalypse. But after a few hours study, he learned exactly why Jaden was quick to tell him. The Manifest of Apocalypse was supposedly written several billion years ago by a person named Xatrial Isenhart, who held the title known as Universal Defender, itself an honorific given to beings who alongside dealing with and fighting the most dangerous existential threats to the universe, tend to sort out fair play across the cosmos as well. Xatrial, however, was the one among these Defenders who few remember. A consequence of being the defender of a relatively peaceful universe. Even so, Xatrial was plagued by visions of doom that he would not be around to see, let alone stop. Thus, he had written the Manifest of Apocalypse before his death that no one actually knows the details of.

The book itself contained Xatrial's many theorized ways that all time and space could end, as well as how to stop them. At least, that's what the legend said. The information pertinent to the now was the idea that the Manifest of Apocalypse had been found. At least, quite possibly.

Miles piloted his ship to a solar system containing three worlds known as the Strife Planets: Zharekk, Kalivan Tor, and Raon-Arashal. The Manifest allegedly rested within a great bastion on Zharekk called Soulshatter Keep. The local Vulpians of the Death World variety (that were technically known as the Zharekai Vulpians, but were physically and ideologically similar to Death Worlders of Raon-Arashal) had built an outpost village not far from Soulshatter Keep. Miles met with one of the local guidesmen, by the name of Moldrenor.

"Miles Radien, I came on the trail of a message from Jaden of Laksor!" Miles introduced himself, his voice able enough to cut through the howling winds.

"Good to meet you, Miles!" Moldrenor greeted. "This outpost is still rather under construction, but we're not really counting on it to become a settlement! Hence our lack of a weather shield!"

Both men had to raise their voices considerably to make themselves clear. While not outright gales, the wind was strong indeed. The two walked towards the outer walls of the outpost overlooking the walls of Soulshatter Keep.

"How do we know that this is the resting place of the Manifest of Apocalypse?" Miles asked. "My contact's information seemed unsure of even itself!"

"Right now, it's mostly because of just how devious these traps are in that castle!" Moldrenor explained. "The architecture and age is also from the correct Era and species, and if there's anywhere a guy like Xatrial would've left a book like the Manifest, it would be here!"

"Traps?" Miles inquired.

"Aye! The fort's crawling with 'em! Scan-Pulses can hardly count just how many mines are in front of the place, let alone how to disable them!"

"Well, it sounds like you just need someone who can get in and get out, avoiding the traps instead of asking the stars for a nice and clean yellow brick road!"

Moldrenor stopped for a moment, trying to figure out the metaphor. But Miles pressed forth, soon at the vista that allowed him to behold Soulshatter Keep. A massive stone castle of silvery grey, and it just *felt* dense. Like the roads of a highway town, driven across over decades without a single accident, and all the cars and bikes and footsteps made it seem even more solid than when it was first poured into place and set. It wasn't even an extravagant-looking castle, either. Large, to be sure. But to call the place a Keep seemed a misnomer. More like... above-ground bunker. Just this giant rectangular prism of stone, with clearly much more priority given to what was to be held within than any outward appearance.

Miles's initial attempt to use The Aura's sight was met with a screeching sort of feedback, there was just too much information for him to process anything useful out of it.

"Damn, that wasn't a trait of Xatrial, was it?" Miles asked as Moldrenor caught up with him.

Moldrenor shrugged. "Not sure. If there was ever a forgotten Defender, it was Xatrial Isenhart."

"It shows."

"Look, given enough time, we *can* figure out what's where, how to disable it correctly, and do it. No one has to risk a bone in their body."

"My patience is of a very specific kind," Miles replied as he did a few limbering-up kicks, which were mostly just swinging his entire leg up and down in different ways to stretch the muscles a little. "This is not one of those kinds."

Carefully making his way down the overlook hill, Miles kept The Aura's sight in a state of revealing anything trap-like within fifteen meters of him, and getting past the minefield in front of Soulshatter Keep-But-More-Like-Bunker-Honestly became simply a matter of stepping just between their trigger radiuses. The path he was taking had an oddly deliberate feel, clearly Xatrial designed the fields to be navigated by the memory of someone who planted all these devices. To the long-deceased Defender's credit, cosmic powers and technology in the universe wouldn't have been able to detect the mines buried here like Miles was able to now.

Meanwhile at the camp, Moldrenor watched from afar with some binoculars.

"Well, it's working," Moldrenor commented.

"So would doing this safely, eventually," a Kanikai from the camp muttered. Not disdainfully, just doubting the necessity of what Miles was doing.

"I get the feeling a guy like him prefers to be actively involved."

A moment passed in awkward silence.

"Okay, that was the wrong way to say it, but I don't have a solid wording yet. Gimme a break," Moldrenor tentatively corrected himself.

Soon enough, Miles was inside the Keep-Technically-Bunker-But-Who's-Actually-Keeping-Score, making his way through the halls, strangely devoid of traps. One could suppose this is where it was more earning the name of a fortress or castle. The interior of Soulshatter Keep wasn't loomingly spacious, but comfortably so. An equilibrium between a vast openness that one could appreciate, without crossing the line to flat-out intimidating or foreboding. A hermit's dream, this place was. Miles even considered asking Moldrenor how he might just make this fort his own, despite his already existent home on Cynofrax. The house on Cynofrax was a home, no doubt, but Soulshatter Keep was the kind of place you'd have at the end of an adventure game, where all the trophies and medals of your achievements and exploits were displayed, and where the most powerful weapons you acquired in your journey sat upon racks in a dedicated armory, where you would reminisce of how you acquired them, and the times you used them. Where you'd keep your library, of the many books you read, wrote, and learned from. Miles couldn't think of the word to describe it, but Soulshatter Keep was definitely it.

But that would have to come later, if at all. Speaking of libraries, Miles needed to find the Manifest of Apocalypse, and that was likely the best place to start. And yes, Soulshatter Keep did possess a library that Miles was able to find handily enough.

While there were many eye-catching and curiosity-arousing titles present, such books as "They Called Him

Doom", "The Madman of Terevetz", and "Chosen in Name", the volume Miles sought wasn't present. Out of curiosity, though, Miles grabbed the volume "They Called Him Doom". But when he opened the book, it was empty. This thing had to be over a thousand pages long, but there was nothing written in it. Flipping through to confirm this, Miles did find a single line of text somewhere around page six hundred.

He was doom.

"I really don't know what I expected," Miles commented, returning the tome to its place on the shelf. Then he realized something.

"If Xatrial wrote the Manifest himself, he wouldn't have kept it in his library. The library's where you keep the ideas that weren't yours to start," Miles realized, heading into what he sure hoped was the study. As much as it would only make sense for the adjoining room to be a study, it might not have been the same standard for the Loriken that Xatrial was.

Sure enough, it was a study. It was oddly immaculate and well-organized for a being who's one solid reputation was the visions of doom he'd be unable to help fight. Maybe he handled it better than one might expect. Miles opened the drawer in the desk itself, and beheld an ancient tome, still laced with power to stop it from decaying. Even though it didn't look older than a decade, it sure felt like its age.

On the End of All Things: A Manifest of the Apocalypse I am doomed to not fight

This was Xatrial's musings, all right. Miles opened the book carefully, purely out of curiosity. The first page looked like it was written after all the other ones, for some reason.

When I first began writing in this journal, I intentionally left this first page blank, that when all others are filled, I may return to this one and tell of my cruel understanding, that whoever reads this might better comprehend what they are about to read. I am Xatrial Isenhart, Loriken. I bear the title of Universal Defender, like four others before me. But unlike these men and women, I live in a time of calmness for the universe. My predecessor ended the Demon War, and secured many artifacts too powerful to be present in the universe at large, locking them away in the vault I now guard as his successor. My contributions, while not none, are likely fewer than any other who will bear this title will be. But that has not stopped my nightmares. Visions of doom that plague me constantly, and taunt me mercilessly with my knowledge that I will be long gone from the worlds before they have the chance to manifest themselves.

This has not stopped me from preparing, though. This is my Manifest of Apocalypse. Every nightmare I have had, and how to defeat it when I am not around to do it myself. There are so many ways that the stars themselves can burn, that the worlds can be turned to ash. I did not have all of them dancing in my head cruelly, but I did have many. I hope that these... ravings, as they may seem, will one day be what I contribute to the safety of all worlds, and the peoples upon them.

I will not despair that 'glory was stolen from me'. It is folly. I suppose someone needed to be the one with all the time to plan, but never the chance to act. If all this planning, then, leads to the act of someone, maybe a future Defender saving all reality... That will be my victory.

—Xatrial Isenhart, Loriken of Sharaeine

That would explain why the first page seemed like it was written last. It was. Clever idea, Miles admitted to himself before taking the book to an exit hatch.

The tunnel the hatch led to put him on the other side of the valley from the camp, and when Miles exited, the tunnel appeared to fill itself in with dirt and sand. Not even collapse, just fill itself. Illusion or not, it was likely easier to have done what he just did, even if this route was known of. Either way, he had Xatrial's Manifest, and just needed to head back to Moldrenor's camp.

On his way, Miles flipped through the tome, wondering if there was a version of his Opponent Unbeatable described in here. That nightmare of his own, maybe Xatrial had similar. While there were a few types of 'superdemon' the Manifest talked about, none of them quite fit the bill of the Opponent Unbeatable. Didn't hurt to try, though.

"I get the feeling this guy would've done a hell of a lot if it weren't for his existential timing," Miles commented as he delivered the Manifest to Moldrenor. He then paused as he processed what he just said. "Story of my fuckin' life right there…"

"I'm sure there's a terribly clever reply to that, I just don't know what it is," Moldrenor replied, and Miles nodded with an enthusiastic 'fair enough'. "I wonder, though…"

The Zharekai Vulpian seemed to have his doubts as he held Xatrial's writings. "All the ways Xatrial figured reality could end, right? He planned how to stop them all. But the thing is, this book, by its nature, details how to end reality in a lot of ways."

Miles listened.

"I mean, our initial plan was to, well, get this transcribed into a bunch of different languages and have basically a copy at just about every planet-level library we can get them to, so that people are prepared, right? But that's a lot of people knowing a lot of ways all creation could get completely… just done for."

"I think I understand what you're getting at," Miles said. "Especially with the humans out and about in the universe now, there's definitely an aspect of 'can't have nice things' that shouldn't be ignored."

"Humans or not, I just can't justify this book's passages being common knowledge. But I sure as hell can't say it needs to be exclusive. I mean, what the hell do you do with that sort of situation? This is vital stuff here! But it's also a step-by-step how to just wreck everything in a million different ways!"

Both Miles and Moldrenor pondered intensely as the Manifest sat on the table between them in Moldrenor's tent.

"One copy, this one alone," Miles said, forming his plan aloud. "People can know it exists. They can know that it's secured. That someone's keeping it safe. If anything comes up, and someone's got the slightest inkling that it's in here, they have the right to figure that out. Until it's needed, it's not needed."

Moldrenor pieced it together, and Miles seemed to do so as well. "Turazin," they both said simultaneously. Soon enough, the Manifest was in Turazin's archive, under Xenidar's guard.

"I mean, solid plan, guys," Xenidar noted after hearing their story. "I'll get to transcribing it into the Hideout's system, make stopping the end of reality a little more streamlined, as it were."

Moldrenor nodded, and thanked Xenidar before heading out, likely back to Zharekk.

"So, what's on your mind now?" Xenidar asked. Miles was about to open his mouth when it was suddenly added "And if you tell me 'nothing' or anything like that, I'll punch your kneecaps straight off."

"Right," Miles said, though not downplaying the uniqueness of Xenidar's threat. "It's a sort of quiet, nagging thought that doesn't even have any words, but just exists."

Xenidar seemed to understand what that meant, somehow.

"Like, I don't know what I'm doubting, how it's being doubted or anything like that. But there's definitely something just... existing there, letting me know that there's something, all right."

Xenidar hopped into his chair, and started typing something. Likely the machine command for the transcription of the Manifest of Apocalypse. "Y'know Radien, I don't think I need to tell you that you have those instincts for a reason. But I probably should tell you that with your power, those instincts get a lot more reliable. Not necessarily more potent or sharpened, but more reliable for sure."

Miles nodded slightly, and turned around to leave.

"With the backing of The Aura, it's a much worse idea than usual to pass those off," Xenidar reiterated, then continued working.

Miles returned to Cynofrax, and prepared some soup for the purpose of eating it in the darkness. He had started to perfect the recipe, figuring out more and more just what goes into the kind of soup you eat alone, in the darkness.

"Once I really get this figured out and written down, I'm gonna call it 'soup for the darkness.'" He said to himself, sitting down with two bowls, and closing his eyes, summoning the effigy again.

"I never really had a proper name for you, did I?" Miles started. "I've understood you to be 'me but stronger' and what have you, but there was never a short version of it. I mean, I guess your name is Miles Sorvenjar Radien. But that's beside the point."

Miles slurped some of his soup, it was rather hard for him not to slurp, given a cleft lip from birth. His facial hair rather well hid the scar, though.

"Y'know, I think one of the main reasons I can hardly believe this all is because it's what I've wanted. And in a strange way, too. Like... 'I didn't know I wanted it this way, but clearly I do.'"

Miles constructed the next part of the thought in his head. He knew what he wanted to say, how to say it just needed to catch up.

"I never would've thought that the universe is full of really cool-looking and cool-acting peoples. I mean, Vulpians and Redarians? Who wouldn't want to hang out with Fox People and Red Panda people? And I'm not strange to the *idea* of species like that, I just might not have immediately had those names for them. The worlds in my head, that I've imagined as I played on my own as a kid... They never looked like these ones, but they *could've*. I very well could have imagined this stuff eventually."

Miles then sipped his drink, this time it was a strong one, given that the soup was actually pretty hearty.

"It's hard to believe that I occupy a universe that I'd want to. But I remember what the Prism said, I definitely spent way too long on Earth."

CHAPTER THE SIXTEENTH

After he dismissed the effigy, Miles just sat at the table, two empty bowls that once held soup in front of him.

"I do stand alone," he admitted to himself. "But that's not a bad thing."

As soon as he stood up, however, Miles found himself in the swirling red vortex of his old nightmare.

"No, not again!" he yelled, waiting for the Opponent Unbeatable to show itself. The land tore away around him, and he just stood there, waiting.

"Come on, you son of a bitch. Let's get this over with!" Miles challenged. "I know how this works, now hurry it up!"

<TODAY I SAVE MYSELF>

The Opponent did not come as it normally did, however. Instead, the whole world seemed to glitch out around him, the crimson winds stuttering and faltering, and the vision ended.

"I was too ready," Miles postulated. "It wasn't getting the drop on me. I was ready to have the nightmare again, which rather defeats its purpose."

A moment passed before his next conclusion.

"I'll take it," Miles scoffed confidently. "It means I beat it a little bit this time. And I will take that."

It gave Miles a lot to ponder. He made the Opponent Unbeatable retreat. This was new. Though he understood it would surely return at some point, Miles had a base to build on: He knew how it worked. The Opponent Unbeatable would show itself, and make Miles look weak. But Miles was ready for it to do that, and thus the Opponent couldn't send its message.

"But what is the next step of this?" he asked himself as he paced in his home. "There's one to be found for sure, but what is it?"

He understood something about the Opponent Unbeatable, which meant that it *could* be beaten. Without its absolute nature, it could not do its deed, it could not go through its paces.

"Understanding," Miles concluded. "That's its weakness. I understood. I just need to understand more.

No, not more... just something else as well. There is an understanding that can break this thing. I just know it. There is something that if I came to understand it, the Opponent Unbeatable is surely doomed."

The only question that remained was the question of what needed be understood. What was this fact that Miles had to discover, determine, and accept? Though he wasn't exactly pressed for time to figure it out, sooner would be better than later. Taking his ship to Turazin, Miles found a terminal within The Hideout to search the Grand Database for any writings or accounts similar to the Opponent Unbeatable. The universe is a big place, surely he couldn't be the first to have this nightmare.

Initially, it seemed there was a cornucopia of information on how to defeat this shadow, but as Miles narrowed the search terms more and more by what existed in the vision, there became less and less to show for it. Probably for the better, Miles figured, he didn't want to sift through a mountain of musty old tomes depicting all the nightmares of the stars, and pick out only a few tidbits from it all.

There was one thing, one eerily similar account written by Alikos Teyn, a member of a now-extinct species known as the Kendrosians. Apparently, one of the oldest species in the universe, wiped out by Caltoran after his corruption. The end of the peoples of

Kendrossos was one of the most devastating blows the universe had ever suffered, and many still today mourned the fall of a very wise, proud and populous race.

Though the Kendrosian genocide certainly is no matter to be glossed over in any regard, the diary of Alikos Teyn mentioned 'a creature of crimson shade, whom no strike can harm,' which was almost spot-on for the Opponent Unbeatable, though he referred to it as a more a reaper-type being, the manifest of death's inevitability.

Unfortunately, the journal of Alikos Teyn was not entirely within The Hideout's Grand Database. It had not been fully transcribed, much to Miles's chagrin.

"Xenidar, where's the physical instance of the journal of Alikos Teyn?" Miles asked him at his desk, to which the short, stocky Talvas Vulpian leaned back with an 'urrrgh' noise as he tried to recall. He raised a single finger, he seemed about to remember.

"Underground, B32. Section... 9, Case 13. I don't remember which row, but there's a labelplate," he finally answered.

Miles nodded, and headed to the elevator. "B32, Section 9," Miles stated as his destination, to the confirming beep of the elevator.

Miles stepped out and made his way to Case 13, which essentially was 'bookcase 13'. The underground library that took up almost the entire planet's mantle was organized in such a way that B-floors 30-90 were exclusively for literature written by the Kendrosian species. Hard copies of just about every book, even the most common ones, just in case. Floor B32 was for personal journals of noted Kendrosians, section 9 was just where Alikos Teyn's ended up.

On the shelf was actually two volumes, the original handwritten journal of a well-renowned weaponsmith for the purpose of preserving, and a copy for the purpose of viewing. Miles grabbed the latter, given that the former was in a protective case, that definitely had an alarm on it.

Flipping to the page where Alikos Teyn described his reaper, Miles studied.

A crimson shade, who no strike can harm. That is the appearance of a strange new doom that haunts my dreams. I know I am not physically weak, nor untrained. But I cannot make this accursed being die, no matter where or how I make my assault. I believe this is an image of death, its inevitability made manifest. One cannot fight death itself, let alone win. But death seems not the kind to taunt, as this invulnerable creature does with its existence, and its actions, or lack thereof, rather.

"Ok, but how to beat it?" Miles asked aloud.

I have tried many methods, even entering my dreamscape with weapons of both my creation, and others. Yet this shade remains indestructible, and seems keen to drive me to madness in my fruitless quest to fight it.

UDM 8-317M - I encountered the shade again, but simply did not fight it this time. I stood and waited for what it would do, as I knew I could not destroy it. The being also stood before me, staring me down, as if challenging me. But I knew I couldn't destroy it by any means I could muster, so I awaited its action. It did nothing, and even seemed frustrated at my lack of fight. At least, as frustrated as a blood-red shadow creature without a face can appear to be. I now understood that it could be beaten, even if only by my refusal to try. But that seemed to weaken it. It was physically smaller on my next encounter. Though it still stood well over me in height, it wasn't by as much as usual. My curiosity got the better of me, and I attempted combat again. It defended itself, to my surprise. It had never done that before. It normally allowed me to strike it endlessly, to no avail. But this meant I had weakened it by understanding that it could be beaten. That said, it still bested me in combative skill, stamina and durability. Perhaps there is something else that will allow me to fight it more effectively. A knowledge or understanding that it cannot beat.

UDM 8-317M, ent. 2 - It has been several months since my last entry, and I have pondered intensely for most of it. There have been moments where it has returned to full strength as I tried to fight it, and failed. But then I'd simply understand that I couldn't outfight it, and its inability to fight me led to its weakening. I have reflected as well upon my own life, wondering if there is a reason I see this specter. I did not lead the most ambitious of youths, despite what my current experience of life may suggest. In fact, the opposite. Mine was an upbringing of stagnation broken only by failure of endeavor, and utter lack of opportunity to prove myself. I don't know if even I desired then or now to prove myself to anyone other than myself. To at least understand that I, Alikos Teyn, can be as I so wish, and can call myself warrior. But I understand that I trained. I understand that I am not physically weak, yet this being is unconvinced. There must be something else. There must be something I can know about myself and accept that will spell the doom of this evil shade, if even it is evil, over simple maliciousness.

The remaining entries simply detailed Alikos Teyn's many hypotheses, none of them proving true. But apparently, the Opponent Unbeatable one day simply stopped showing up in his dreams. It inexplicably just... ceased to haunt him, and he never figured out why. The final words in the journal were from his deathbed.

I die old, and fulfilled in many ways but one. I never did know what that shadow in my prime was. I cannot fathom why it went away. Why it didn't even fade, but just disappeared altogether. There was no development that could warrant this, and I become tired, weary as I write this, desperately hoping that my writing of this account will grant me my final epiphany. I don't know why... why did it leave... I am so weary, but I must understand... there still is an understanding... Did I defeat it? Am I victorious in the end? I... the creature, no, he appears! Not now, not at my final doom! Doom upon it, it should have been! I had won! I had won! It went away, and I was the victor! I understood that for all that time!

...

The creature fades... I am victorious at last.

"That was... almost exceptionally dark," Miles commented, before shelving the journal. "But somehow I doubt that it's gonna disappear for me until my final day. Alikos Teyn only had this thing show itself in the middle of his life, I've been haunted for as long as I can remember. But there is no doubt: Understanding indeed."

But the part where he had reflected on his youth… stagnation, failure in endeavor, and no chance to prove himself, to himself more than any other. A feeling Miles had all his life, but didn't have the words for until he saw the writings of a Kendrosian weaponsmith.

As he made his way home, Miles kept putting the pieces together. They were all falling into place. When Miles had first been introduced to this wider universe, the Opponent Unbeatable was nowhere. These first few years where he hadn't had the nightmare, even if only because he wasn't sleeping. He hadn't even thought of the Opponent Unbeatable in that time. It wasn't like he had forgotten it ever troubled him, there was just so much of everything else happening that the Opponent Unbeatable couldn't even be on his mind. But only recently, as things calmed down, only recently as he started to wonder if he'd have to wake up…

He walked through the door of his house, he was ready for a breakthrough.

In that time before the Opponent Unbeatable returned, he understood that he was getting his worlds! The worlds in his head that he now got to visit, he understood that was real! The Opponent showed up in the lull, where Miles had the time to doubt! But Miles knew himself well, and knew he couldn't just tell himself it was real and believe it... no, something had to truly prove to him that he wasn't going to wake up, because there was no dream to awaken from! Something had to tell him...

"People can misinterpret, people can fail to understand. But powers don't lie. The Aura isn't something that can lie. It's a power, a fact of the universe. It can't have an ulterior motive or a 'different experience' in the traditional sense." The Prism's voice said Miles's own words to him in his head.

Miles stood there, on the brink of victory or defeat, only time would tell.

"There is a reason my voice does not come from a throat. Why the whispers of The Aura have no body they are whispered from. It is The Aura's promise of its own existence. A power, that is not a lie, but a fact. One can lie about fact, but the fact shall always remain, a fact!"

Miles's resolve steeled a thousandfold. "Then Aura guide me, through friend and foe alike, that I may emerge in great victory!!"

The ground tore itself away again, forming its arena, the swirling red hurricane its borders. The Opponent emerged once again from the edge of doom, and moved with dark purpose towards Miles.

"Not this time," Miles said, snapping his fingers and at last creating a bright blue flame of The Aura. "The universe does not lie."

The Opponent drew closer, faster than usual, but with a palpable air of desperation, a dire attempt to regain its power over Miles.

"The Aura is of the universe, a power that cannot be a lie!" Miles declared, throwing the bolt at the Opponent, which caused the evil shade to stagger. Though it had no visage, there was no mistaking: it was shocked. Truly taken aback by Miles's power over it, instead of the other way around.

Miles fired another bolt, this time punching a fist-sized hole in its body. Another, and one of the Opponent's legs was blown off, scattering into nothingness. Now, to finish it. Miles dropped back into a stance, one he'd never use in a fight. But to conjure a great sphere of azure energy, swirling and flashing with power? This was its purpose.

"You are defeated!" Miles declared, and with a great heave of his entire body, Miles propelled the blast forward towards its quarry with his left hand, leaving it extended as the orb of power barreled towards an opponent doomed. The explosion engulfed the landscape around him, turning the once red arena blue, and the wailing walls of wind calmed and dissipated as the Cynofrax around him returned to normal, and he stood once again in his home. Only one thought in his mind, that became voice.

"Today, I have saved myself."

PLANETARY GLOSSARY

Cynofrax — The origin planet of the Vulpian species, Cynofrax is also the resting place of the Aura Prism, a sentient manifest of cosmic power that holds the barriers between reality and the Burning Hells. Though the barriers are not impenetrable, they are able to ensure that Demons do not walk freely within the universe, and that incursions are exceptionally uncommon. Cynofrax also acts as a cultural hub for much of the generally united universe, and central planet for just about everything else, including trade, research, and developments within. Most of the planet's habitable surface is known as Sectora Neutros, the landmass dotted with self-governed towns and cities that, while by definition independent, still give their allegiance to Cynofrax as a whole, and will stand together in crisis. Cynofrax is also home to the Arenaland province, in which willing participants enter a pseudo-virtual reality where they inhabit a copy of their body within the area and the entire province, about the size of Portugal is an open combat zone. This allows people to train lethally without actually dying, but in the event their avatar is killed, a person is required to take a minimum two-week away from Arenaland as they recover from the surreal nature of 'dying but not really.'

Orvitaire — Orvitaire is known as the Martial Planet, having been founded by Loriken warriors, philosophers and other free-thinkers and free-acters as a means of escaping an incredibly bureaucratic time in neighboring planet Sharaeine's history. The planet hadn't quite reached the level of needing to fill out a form to get government permission to go to the store, but it certainly was at the level of needing government permission to be successful as a person. The warrior side of the equation of

Orvitaire's founders were in the majority, as sport and competition on the Loriken homeworld had been regulated to the point of maliciousness, as if the entire planet had been taken over by the Concerned Mother's Brigade(TM), so to speak. Orvitaire is and has always been a planet of fighters and warriors, and the unofficial collective motto is "To be stronger warriors, and better peoples."

Turazin — Home of both the Conclave of Sentience and The Hideout (along with its Grand Database), Turazin is seen widely as an incredibly important planet for the cause of the general unity of most of the universe. General unity, in this sense, being mostly 'communicable' more than anything else. The Conclave of Sentience is not a governing body, and the only law they actually implement and enforce is the non-interference law when it comes to species not officially recognized as sentient, but that clearly are, and have yet to finish their development to the point of contact. The Conclave mostly acts as moral guidance for most of the universe, essentially being the beacons of 'best practices,' with their rulings (but honestly more like determinations) on the

Essential Uncompromising Rights of sentient species (which boil down to access to food, water, shelter, communications, medicine, right to equal and unbiased protection under law, and right to self-defense), and the common decency 'law' known as Spirit of the Stone (which is basically the law of 'don't be shitty'), among others.

Redaria Prime – Redaria Prime is the homeworld of the Redarian species, even though they originated from neighboring Redaria Omega. Homeworld and the term "Capitol World" are rather interchangeable. Regardless, Redaria Prime is home to Alstralzin, or more colloquially "The City of Progress", wherein the sciences see some of their most significant developments in the modern universe. Initially this title was more earned on Redaria Omega's city of Falko-Rakara, but while Redaria Omega's scientific community is certainly nothing to sniff at, Alstralzin has rather replaced it in reputation over relatively recent times.

Redaria Omega – Though certainly not a lawless or hostile world, the Redarian origin planet is decidedly more rough around the edges. It is on this planet that more controversial scientific methods and scientists find their home, if only because it is significantly harder to enforce common decency regulations on Redaria Omega than Redaria Prime, given that Redaria Omega is significantly larger as a planet, hence. Redaria Omega's two moons, however, are the haven of 'black market science' as it were, and even most on Redaria Omega would rather not deal with the methods employed in the name of science on the moons of Aldin and Virak.

Talvakorrik – Sometimes referred to as 'the beating mechanical heart of the galaxies,' Talvakorrik is the planet the Talvas Vulpian species hails from. Being one of the three major descendants of the Old Cynofraxian species (The others being the Cynofrax and Death World Vulpians), Talvas Vulpians are essentially the dwarves of the lot, almost quite literally. An adult Talvas Vulpian rarely stands above four feet tall, and as a species, they are very mechanically inclined. Some of the best engineers the stars have known were Talvas Vulpians. They have generally shied away from weapons tech, save for a few notable examples

(Such as the AZP-621 Multi-Munition Pistol), preferring instead to machinery in ships, power generation and architecture, leaving the weaponsmithing to their cousins, the Dor-Val-Der Vulpians.

Pogo-Pira – Pogo-Pira is the origin planet and homeworld of the Hydenti and Hykentiu species, though few Hydenti actually remain in existence, a consequence of natural evolution and genetic offshooting. One of the many planets in the universe with far more water than land, much of Pogo-Pira's species, particularly the sentient ones, started as aquatic life before inevitably evolving amphibious capability. Pogo-Pira is one of the few water-majority planets that gains significant tourism and visitation for just about any other reason, as many land-base species have a tendency to be slightly unnerved by Pogo-Pira's underwater cities, and there is a common condition generously named "Landstrider's Nervewrecker" that is essentially what happens when someone from a land-favoring species has a nervous breakdown in one of Pogo-Pira's underwater towns and the like. It's not as prevalent as it used to be, as at least 90% of Pogo-

Pira's sentient population lives underwater.

Caren'Das – The homeworld/capitol world of the Hajivakk species, Caren'Das acts as a major trade hub for the communicable universe, being a larger than average planet with six moons of decent size. Naturally, there's a lot of space on Caren'Das. Both it and the rest of the Nashira Strand solar system have seen their fair share of conflict, being as central a planetary system as it is.

Laksor – The homeworld and origin planet of the Laksorian species (obviously), Laksor has earned a mixed reputation across most of the universe, and one's opinion on the planet as a whole largely depends on how acceptable they find brothels. Though not Laksor's dominant feature, as the planet also has a very strong scientific and philosophical community, and while Laksor isn't the only planet to have them, their most prominent feature is how much they charge for services, or rather, the fact that they don't.

Gliropa – Though a mainly Hykentiu planet, Gliropa doesn't have as large an underwater population as Pogo-Pira, located in the same solar system (or

Celestial Array, as the common term is in most places). As such, some have referred to Gliropa as "Pogo-Pira lite", but that is slightly a misnomer. It's more like "If Pogo-Pira wasn't mostly underwater", if that makes any regard of sense. Gliropa is considered 'a strangely average planet,' as its history, while not uneventful, isn't enormously significant, and the same can be said of its cities and landscape. This would likely make Gliropa a hidden gem for tourists, if any of those smart travelers decided to spill those beans.

Mjarfus (Pronounced Myar-fuss) – Despite only very brief mentioning, Mjarfus is the origin planet of the Hajivakk people, and, while being the center of Haji-Son culture in many ways, is quite cold as a planet. Most of Mjarfus's solar years are a constant state of winter, but never quite 'dead of winter'. This gave rise to the phrase 'There is always snow on the grounds of Mjarfus, but its cold never stings' which usually means something along the lines of 'Something might look harsh on the surface, but is actually quite fair, and the appearance weeds out the unworthy.' This phrase did fall out of favor. It may have risen, but has recently fallen, much to the relief of many species who aren't fond of metaphors. Snowball Combat is a very prominent sport on Mjarfus, hosting regular tournaments on both regional and planetary scale. The largest of these tournaments is often opened by the Exemplar themselves.

Alabasteron – Colloquially referred to as "The Graveworld", Alabasteron is decidedly the planet that had the most battles upon its surface during the Sentience War. The entire planet is scarred moors, and the ancient skeletons of warriors from long ago still constantly fight each other, but cannot die. The consensus has generally been that those on Alabasteron at the time fought with fury and passion such that not even death could quell their will. None dare set foot upon the shattered planet these days, given that there's no real reason to, and that they'd rather not be caught in the crossfire between indestructible warring factions.

Bol'Drakkin – Though many different types of Dragon species exist in the universe (referred to as Genetic Castes), the Bol'Drakkin Draconians are the most numerous, and their home world is Bol'Drakkin itself. Among the Dragons of

Bol'Drakkin, there exists clan-families known as Battle Brothers. The main difference between Bol'Drakkin Battle Brother Families and traditional clan structure is that one has absolutely zero need to be born into them. In fact, the main way these Battle Brother Families gain members is Dragons (and other species sometimes, if they're into that sort of thing) simply ask to be allowed in, after which a test is administered, and often passed. The morals and values of Battle Brother Families are easily attainable knowledge, and joining them is usually a matter of one's own values aligning. For example, one of the more prominent Battle Brother Families, the Jurovendr, they hold the motto of "Though honor is luxury before right, ours is to do well by the worlds," and another well-known Battle Brother Family, the Veyret-Kai believe, "Strength through skill at arms, all of them". The Veyret-Kai are well known as warriors and academics.

Raon-Arashal – Often called "The Devouring Jungle", Raon-Arashal is the home world of the Death World Vulpians, decidedly the more warrior-like Vulpian species between their Cynofraxian and Talvakorrik cousins. Death Worlders hold survival skills in high regard, electing to send themselves for up to weeks at a time into the planet's "Black zones", areas where the natural environment is so hostile, one Loriken researcher called these zones "The kind of place the reaper might not want to bother with for fear of his own continued life". Permanent cities do exist on Raon-Arashal, such as Firatyne and Kendradeyne, but still many choose to hone their skills in this ultimate test. In fact, some elite militaries in the universe train their special forces in Raon-Arashal's Black Zones.

Zharekk – Even with Zharekk not as naturally hostile a place to live as Raon-Arashal, the Zharekai Vulpians are not to be overlooked when compared to the Death Worlders they descended from. The planet of Zharekk is well known as having some of the most potent tornadoes and windstorms for several galaxies, and in fact, more settlements and cities on Zharekk use weather-shielding technologies than neighboring Raon-Arashal. Zharekk has also been historically, a popular place to exile oneself to, as many bunkers and fortresses dot the planet, that warriors both ancient and modern had chosen to spend their days in solitude in.

Sharaeine (Pronounced Sha-rain) – The Loriken origin planet of Sharaeine has had a rather turbulent history, much to the chagrin of its people nowadays. All the way from not long after the Demon War of the Third Cosmic Era, the planet has had many regimes ranging from the bureaucratic to the tyrannical, to the incredibly flawed as a direct result of an immediately prior tyrannical regime. Even now, in what is considered the 'modern' universe, Sharaeine and its peoples still struggle with progressive ideals, due to many on the planet simply being too paranoid that something new and bad is going to happen again, as it were. Many people, Loriken and otherwise who leave the planet for brighter prospects are rather reluctant to divulge the fact they came from Sharaeine, due to its reputation, and the reasons it exists.

Kalivan Tor – The Strife Planets are three: Zharekk, Raon-Arashal, and Kalivan Tor. Not much is actually known about this planet, or its reclusive Vulpians, referred to as the Siivalar. Kalivan Tor is home to one of the few collective societies that have successfully lived underground, its necessity stemming from the high surface temperatures on much of the planet, given its proximity to the parent star of the system. In their few dealings with the outside universe, Siivalar Vulpians have shown a rather odd sort of inherent Psionic tendencies. Because while Cynofrax Vulpians have themselves latent Psionic power, the Siivalar Vulpians have a disposition to "Burst-type" power-wielding, i.e., short bursts of exceptionally potent raw power, a Psionic 'style' that many had believed to have fallen out of relevancy long ago.